P9-DEX-762

Black Elk in Paris

Black Elk in Paris

A NOVEL

KATE HORSLEY

TRUMPETER
Boston & London
2006

TRUMPETER BOOKS
An imprint of Shambhala Publications, Inc.
Horticultural Hall
300 Massachusetts Avenue
Boston, Massachusetts 02115
www.shambhala.com

9 8 7 6 5 4 3 2 1

FIRST EDITION
Printed in the United States of America

♾ This edition is printed on acid-free paper that meets the American National Standards Institute z39.48 Standard.
Distributed in the United States by Random House, Inc., and in Canada by Random House of Canada Ltd

Designed by Steve Dyer

Library of Congress Cataloging-in-Publication Data
Horsley, Kate, 1952-
Black Elk in Paris: a novel/Kate Horsley.–1st ed.
p. cm.
ISBN-13 978-1-59030-329-0 (acid-free paper)
ISBN-10 1-59030-329-6
1. Black Elk, 1863-1950–Fiction. 2. Exposition universelle de 1889 (Paris, France)–Fiction. 3. Americans–France–Fiction. 4. Paris (France)–Fiction. 5. Oglala Indians–Fiction. I. Title.
PS3558.O6976B57 2006
813'.54–dc22
2005026694

For Aaron

ACKNOWLEDGMENTS

I am grateful to Stephen Pilon, M.D., for his wit and wisdom concerning nineteenth-century French medicine and literature. Melinda Skinner, grammarian and lover of literature, gave the manuscript its first careful read. Kelly McKloskey Romero, French teacher extraordinaire and lover of Paris, purified the French with the help of Annie-Claude Girard. I also thank my friend Professor Paul Gilon for his fierce opinions. Also extremely helpful were the staff and displays at the Musée de l'Assistance Publique and the Musée d'Histoire de la Médecine in Paris. Many valuable books and newspapers were consulted, and I give particular credit for many of the details of Black Elk's life to the book *The Sixth Grandfather: Black Elk's Teachings Given to John G. Neihardt,* edited by Raymond J. DeMallie and published by University of Nebraska Press. Emily Taylor, a Lakota woman, shared important information with me from her own research. Thanks also to Richard Fox, respected colleague and literary gourmet, for being an intelligent reader; and thanks to another esteemed colleague, Frank Melcori, the Italian clown. Victoria Shoemaker remains my worldly and beloved agent, and Beth Frankl is a kind and wise editor whose strengths are too many to list here. I appreciate Katie Keach's good suggestions and DeAnna Satre's crisp editing. Finally, I am grateful to Morgan Davie for his love and support throughout everything.

Black Elk in Paris

1

Je suis un homme raisonnable.

I AM A RATIONAL MAN. My medical education trained me to note and classify the ways in which a man may deteriorate because of hereditary imperfections. I have noted, in myself and others, an odd and illogical inclination to explain the truth away, or even simply not to see it. This seems to me a waste of human reason. But then, what do our emotions do with what we discover, especially when it is this paradox: what the rational mind has led us to see is not, itself, rational.

Thucydides, I learned as a schoolboy, stated that the vulgar take few pains to investigate the truth. Excavating the facts on both sides of his culture's great war between Athens and Sparta, he insisted on the morality of honest, unbiased observation. He did not even trust his own impressions. And he so clearly worships the hero Pericles with an endearing awe that it must have tainted his objectivity. Infatuated with his efforts to see what is, without bias, I launched into my career as a physician. And I have squirreled away books and study the human race's effort to make something of itself through art and literature and society. Sometimes I am amused. Often I teeter between rank cynicism and catatonic angst. But I am functional and respected enough as a physician and scientist. It was Madou who dragged me out of my armchair library and into an empirical test of cultures and perceptions.

It may be an irony that the compelling subject of this document, Mademoiselle Madeleine Balise, often taunted my profession for its inherent futility. She said, "No amount of medicine can make one immortal." I used to defend my career to Madou by stating that a doctor could increase the joy of life by decreasing pain and debilitation. Eventually, she coaxed out of me my own doubts about my profession. It was another incidence of the Indian inspiring a kind of psychic chaos and indiscretion. But I begin my account long after the Indian's departure, when I ran to Salpêtrière, where I had been told that Madou was incarcerated.

When I saw my dear friend shivering like a beggar on one of the wooden chairs of the asylum, I felt particularly ashamed of my profession. Though I admired the institute's esteemed scholar, Dr. Charcot, who, in fact, had been one of my most inspiring mentors, I could not conjure a clinical regard of Madou's delicate hands. I stared at the faint stains of green paint on them as they gripped the edge of the seat. She wavered in my eyes like smoke, a specter from a dream. I had seen so many women displayed by Charcot as specimens of neurological disorders. Just like those other women, Madou's head fell forward, but none had my Madou's brown velvet hair, which even in one of the dim little anterooms of Salpêtrière found some light to hold in a net of curls.

But let me not fall into some sentimental poetic mire. I tell what happened for my own cathartic cure and in order to make a sort of anthropological record of the curious entanglement with Madou and the indigenous American who became her companion, and for whose sake she was put in this madhouse. I was not present at the pivotal occurrence but was told by her sister Clarisse that the catalytic question came from her mother, who said, I was told, "My dear, you are handling your lover's absence with such strength; how do you manage to be so cheerful?" Madou told her something that she would not repeat even to Clarisse. Clarisse reported that Madame Balise just shook her head and repeated in tearful whispers, "She is insane. My little Madou is insane." As she was being kept from leaving their apartment in a chaos of pleading and screaming, Madou called out Choice's name, asking him to stay with her. "It was very sad," Clarisse told me.

Salpêtrière holds a vast number of women who speak to and even fornicate with ghosts as they wash in one of the courtyards or moan in their beds at night. Since my days as a student, the city has encroached upon Salpêtrière so it no longer has its country-estate disguise. The stiff, unembracing stone arms spread out from the domed chapel, an ironic center of a hell realm. A free man, an esteemed colleague, I am able to slip in and out the north door. But I cannot avoid the eyes of the grim statues that seem to narrow as they watch who comes and goes. Many come and never go.

That day when I ran to see Madou, I noted my own physiological symptoms of hysteria: hot skin, gasping, phrases repeating themselves in my head. I entered that sprawling temple of horrors and became another aspect of the muffled swarm of dazed women, doctors, nurses, and a motley staff of attendants. Urgent footsteps, distant yelling, reminded me of my days as a student there, when I believed in the efficacy of observing human pain with clinical detachment. But now the smell of human suffering, a combination of carbolic acid, urine, and damp wood, nauseated me.

I spoke my old friend's name quietly. She seemed asleep to everything but what she saw in her own mind. When she was eleven or twelve and suffering some kind of influenza or stomach upset, I watched her sleeping soundly in a nest of fever. She always regarded her illness as another one of her adventures. A fever fascinated her for its effects on the perception. The physical ailments were insignificant, for Madou, though the youngest, was the strongest of the three Balise sisters. Of all of her family, she was the last I would have predicted to be incarcerated in an asylum. In fact, what compelled me most about Madou was her inordinate good health, a robust deportment that I wanted to sit beside as a man in the desert wants to sit in an oasis. I had already, when I became physician to the Balise family, started to despise the sick.

When she lifted her face to me, I saw in her brown-green eyes the wit and lucidity that her confinement had apparently not snuffed out. I stared at her slightly parted lips, seeing, as a touchstone, that crooked tooth that slanted amongst the others, a whimsical imperfection that was an accessory to her unique beauty. I looked away, and Madou laughed. She had often teased me for not being able to look into another person's eyes for more than a few seconds. But my own eyes might reveal too much, and I had vowed as a young man to refrain from wallowing in impulsive passions, the cloying outbursts that I have often seen expand into destructive chaos in brothels and parlors alike. A great number of my patients in Paris were either the victims or the perpetrators of such impulses. But Madou was not one of those, and so it seemed obscene to see her in a place for hysterics.

"Oh, my dear Tic-Toc," she said, using the nickname that she invented for me when she was a girl and I told her that her heart sounded like a formidable clock. "Can you," she began to say, with a tone that apologized for the trouble she might be making of herself. "Can you take me out of here? They won't let me go." She smiled, showing that distinctive imperfection, that bent tooth. Still trembling, she added, "It is so cold here."

I had no inclination to create a drama with Charcot. I had already insulted him by quitting his Tuesday-evening social dinners. I was certain that the rational thing to do was to wait for some official release, a quiet resolution of the situation that would not further Madou's trauma.

And, in fact, she did not appear as traumatized as I, just very tired, as it is difficult to close one's eyes for a solid sleep when one is surrounded by humans who are expected to do a variety of dark things to themselves and each other. And I knew what the rooms were like where the women were put to bed, the low-ceilinged vaults with two rows of casketlike beds, the sides deep so as to contain a thrashing patient. I sighed and rubbed my face, a habit I have in response to internal confusion.

I bent over and took both her hands in mine. They were, indeed, cold, blood loss in the extremities. My Madou was terrified, and that frightened me.

"No, Madou, it would not be sensible for me to take you out," I told her. "Only your father or the doctors here can determine . . ." Suddenly, I didn't know what might be determined, how one decides when to set another human being free. I looked around me, away from her eyes.

The room was small, one of the waiting rooms outside the amphitheater where medical students listened to lectures on neurological disorders and watched Charcot or one of his colleagues instigate symptoms in some limp woman. I straightened my back, still holding Madou's hands, and she said, "Do you want me to explain . . ."

"No," I said quickly. "No, don't explain to me, Madou. Not now."

She smiled and said, "All right. Not now. I don't want to frighten you."

And all I could think to say was, "Do you need paints?"

She shook her head and whispered, "No." And then

she said, "Will you tell them that I have not been with him since I've been here? Perhaps they will assume that the treatments . . ." She slipped her hands out of mine and looked at the wall beside her as though looking through a window. She said, "So far away."

"Well, you do not belong in here, Madou, and you will be let go soon," I told her. "And, please, don't talk to me as though I'm one of the people who put you here. You have nothing to convince me of." I could not be sure that there was no disease of the tissues, no lesion in her brain, no logic to Madeleine Balise's being in this place. But I wondered how many others of the thousands of women in the asylum were like her, disturbingly free in a society that only pretends to celebrate freedom. She was not a monster.

But there is no place in this society for a spirit who wants neither the fetters of material wealth nor the bondage of some addiction. Perhaps for a while one might claim to be an artist and therefore receive some temporary immunity from social obligations. But eventually, the artists create their own societies with their own conformities and cruel pronouncements of a man's worth. I admit that the power our society has, though in the midst of our simmering terror, is exquisite. This, I believe, is part of what the Indian came to know with such sickening clarity.

Madou considered herself free, the freest of souls. But her great flaw was in wanting the approval and even the admiration of others for her freedom. Many resented her lack of misery. But she found approval and admiration in the Indian's silence, or at least she assumed they were there.

Madou said, "I frightened Father. You know, his nerves . . ."

"Well, yes, he is an easy man to frighten when he is not at his desk in the bank, in the safety of his numbers and ledgers," I said.

Madou laughed and let her head fall back; she moved her hand along her neck as she looked up at the ceiling. I followed that gesture, which always had the ability to disengage me from my theories.

"There is an irony in that, don't you think, Tic-Toc?" she asked. "My father's nerves are damaged and I am being treated for it." Then, looking at me, she added, "I frightened myself, too. I felt that I could die of my emotions, that they were a lethal poison my own body was producing. I was so happy to have him with me when I thought . . . Oh, try to look at me. I won't go on. I shouldn't have told them. I should have lied. I was so content. They sent for you, you know."

"I was in Montmartre, at a burial," I told her, which was true. One of my oldest patients, a venerable veteran of the Prussian War, had died of a cancer of the stomach.

Madou explained, "I was stunned by their response. I remembered when Clarisse was threatened with this place. I only told them the truth. I cannot tell the truth here, can I Philippe?"

I said, "I got the note from Clarisse. I spoke with her."

She rubbed her own arms, holding herself, and said, "It's so cold here."

"It's winter outside," I told her, as though she might have forgotten after the weeks she'd spent inside Salpêtrière.

She continued. "I was trembling and could not articulate any word but 'please.' I lost all dignity. I was so afraid. I do want to leave–as soon as possible."

She laughed again, a quiet amusement at her predicament.

"You know, Tic-Toc, all I was pleading for was for them to understand my happiness. I simply wanted them to understand."

Many times I have felt the same desperation to be understood, and yet I was free to come and go from that huge mausoleum of spirits, a dark stone tomb that looked as benign as a government office or a bank except that there were broken, wide-eyed women inside. I wondered if I would be put in Bicêtre, the men's version of Salpêtrière, if Charcot or any of his colleagues could see into my mind, into my dreams.

"Are you sure that you don't want me to bring you more paints?" was all I could offer.

"No," she answered. "They have put me on the rest cure, you know–that and those wonderful baths, where you are caught like a cow in a vat of heat and your head doused with cold water. I am to rest, except when I am sealed under canvas in scalding water."

She stood up quickly and embraced me as though I were the one who needed comfort.

"Oh, Tic-Toc, don't be so sad," she said. And then, conspiratorially, her mouth close enough so that I could feel the warm breath of her words, which smelled like milk, "He has changed everything, hasn't he? A beautiful man–so very beautiful, like a Greek statue."

And I said, "Yes, Madou," though I knew I was encouraging a romantic imagination that was not healthy for either of us.

2

Comme un homme peut se rendre nécessaire!

HOW NECESSARY a man can make himself! I was family physician to the Balise family for more than twelve years, beginning when Madou was only ten years old and even then a mystery to her mother, who called her "too free." I was twenty-four and full of the arrogance of young doctors. I'd taken over the practice of a Dr. Froulette, who was best known for dispensing opium as a cure for a number of ailments. Several of his clients detested my insistence that opium seemed to cure them because their "sickness" had become an addiction to it. In any case, the Balise family was one of those that required the least medical attention and gave a great deal that a bachelor might appreciate: home-prepared meals and a household dominated by clever young women. At first they lived in the Montmartre district, but this area was still too much of the old Paris, with its circuitous narrow streets and steep climb. Too untouched by Haussmann's grand revisions, Montmartre represented for Monsieur Balise disloyalty to the beloved empire. So he moved his family, when Madou was sixteen, southeastward toward the opera, where they could hear the crowds on the Boulevard des Capucines. It seemed a more fitting location for a banker with marriageable daughters.

Madou was the youngest, a lithe and athletic girl with thick eyebrows on an otherwise delicate face. Her oldest sister, Cecile, was gaunt like her father, and then there was the middle girl, Clarisse, who, I would say, had inherited her mother's easily agitated nerves, though she was the most attractive of the sisters in an obvious way.

I was often asked to various households in Paris for the purpose of being married off to a lingering daughter. More than one husband and several wives, after realizing the entrenched nature of my bachelorhood, told me as though theirs was a unique confession that if they had it to do again, they themselves would not have married. They have congratulated me for maintaining a state free from the infuriating disappointments of romances that try to take refuge in marriage. I did not divulge that I was often lonely. It was a loneliness that never overwhelmed reason, and with my books and music and walking expeditions, I had more of a philosophical melancholy than a corrosive sorrow. There was a sweetness to my solitude, and I found moments of intense passion in it, including those rare moments when what came from my violin actually sounded like what the composer meant to create—at least a bar or two. I also felt an intense lifting away of my loneliness when I encountered a creature of another species in the wild and shared a private moment of intimacy with it. I have had a few of those moments, once when a hawk landed a few feet in front of me as I was resting against the flaky bark of a cedar on a precipice overlooking a long valley in the Parc des Vosges du Nord. I swear the tweed-colored predator did a humorous little dance for me, hopping on one leg and spreading out its wing. When it flew away, I laughed and it answered with a clown's screech.

I do not try to express these experiences to others, for I learned when I was a child that a combination of envy and bitterness can cause others to demean one's passions, and it is easy to demean a man who only dabbles in music when he speaks of the ecstasy of Bach or a man who has dissected dogs when he speaks of a celebration he shared with a hawk one afternoon. It is easier for me to feel love for dead artists and wild animals than to feel love for humans and their domesticated pets. What I feel is a mixture of sorrow and affection for the human race and its childlike efforts to be safe in its skin, which I know all too well will inevitably fail to contain or protect them. I can sometimes see the beauty in their efforts; I often see the ugliness, however, for in addition to my work with the financially secure families, I used to put in a few hours a week with the indigent and the incarcerated. Sometimes I wonder if I did so to remind myself that I am not wrong to avoid the rampant and careless procreative activities that abound where reason would warn against them. Anyone can see the tragedy in the diseases and the hungry children, not to mention the broken arms and bullet wounds that result from the vicissitudes of sexual passions.

Madou's father, Monsieur Balise, once called his youngest daughter a prostitute in my presence. I assured him that he must be a very innocent man to confuse his daughter with one of those women who, from desperation and delusion, attempt to make a living catering to male lust. And in fact Madou laughed heartily and said, "I don't know of any prostitute who is a virgin!" Her mother was scandalized, though in the Paris of today I'm not sure what upset her more, the fact that her husband called their child a prostitute or the fact that her daughter, of twenty then, was a virgin. Madame Balise had a full bosom that seemed more military than sensual, like a padded breastplate on a small general. She spent more time painstakingly fringing her forehead with stiff curls than giving affection to her family, but she was reliable in her routine, which is good for children. Eventually, she, like so many women, found devotion to the church, and to a particularly sentimental young priest, as a way to finally let her passions flower. But that was later, when the whole Balise household, except for the father, was quaking with mysterious longings.

Madou led the way. She could not settle for mediocrity but also abhorred self-indulgent dramas. This put her at odds with most of Paris, in which the wealthy classes were either awash in mediocrity or drowning in self-indulgent dramas. I can see Madame Balise's lips poised over her soupspoon, saying, "Madou is too free; she goes about the city alone too much." But then she looked at me and said, the soupspoon still waiting for her, "Oh, but if she had a good husband, Philippe . . ." She presented the other two girls to me as well, speaking of their qualities, both having interests so perfect for a doctor's wife.

"You are shameless," Monsieur Balise said to his wife. "Dr. Normand is not interested in marriage or he would be fixed up by now. He has that ruddy, Nordic look and a decent enough wardrobe . . . obviously able to finance a family well enough. . . ." He shook his head and returned to sopping up the last of the soup with his bread. His habit in speech was not to finish a sentence, as though it were tedious to supply the obvious conclusion of a thought.

I believe that the greatest hope Madame Balise had in conjunction with her desire to marry one of her daughters off to me was Madou, because, in fact, she and I grabbed opportunities to leave the table as soon as possible and walk together. We sat sometimes on the steps in the Place de la Madeleine, beside that ugliest of churches, though decidedly Greek in its ambitions. Madou admitted many things to me during these walks, including her fear of having a life like either of her sisters.

Madou believed that her sister Clarisse's vitality was being sucked from her by a lover who skillfully kept her in a constant state of insecurity. Clarisse was the sister whom Madame Balise recommended to me on the merits of her interest in medicine, for she had once considered becoming a nurse, and even read medical textbooks, until her man Randolphe became unpleasant about them. Madou called him "the Prince of Darkness."

The oldest sister, Cecile, gave her soul to a little dog she called "Pee-Poo," which she carried around like an infant and which came between her and any suitor as a snarling bundle of curls. The brown stains under its limpid eyes made it seem unhealthy in a contagious way to me. Cecile kissed its head, murmuring her disgust with anything that threatened the dog's thin dignity, including her father, who called the dog a furry tumor. Cecile became a rampant antivivisectionist. Any horrid scientists who mutilated puppies in their evil laboratories deserved her total condemnation. I did not speak out against my colleagues when Cecile listed their sins. And so I was forever the target of either silent or muttered disdain. She kept a protective distance between me and the creature in her arms. Whereas she later thought that the Indian was going to eat Pee-Poo, she was convinced that I would take her pet to some cage and put mercury in its veins. Occasionally, at dinner, Cecile reported on her activities in the Society for the Protection of Animals. She was friends with women like Mademoiselle Bernard, the notorious keeper of more than eighty dogs at her estate, animals rescued from the streets of Paris where concubines' children wasted away unattended, coughing up pieces of their lungs.

I tended to complicate such issues with the truths presented to me by experience. For example, I agreed that the use of animals for experimentation had in many cases burst the bounds of decency; I even agreed that I myself had no stomach for it. But I also knew men whose love and protection of animals were equaled by their horrific mistreatment of humans. I also explained that several studies using animals had proven and specified the toxic effects of some of Paris's most beloved habits. In fact, I suspect the wine merchants of funding these women's heartfelt causes; after all, their precious dogs facilitate research that reveals the hideous toxic effects of wine and other intoxicants.

Any person denouncing alcohol or lust in Paris is accused of being possessed by the soul of an Englishman. Yet Madou did not hide her abstention. Her resistance to hedonism was not so much a moral discipline as a rational recognition of the complete loss of vibrancy and dignity inherent in intoxication and promiscuity. She loved the audacity of the Bohemian crowd but was intensely disappointed in their enslavement to shallow pleasures. She wanted their admiration; she wanted them to take notice of her, for she felt her best chance at companionship was with artists. And she had a horror of mediocrity and saw her sisters as wasting their passions, binding themselves to poodles and maniacal men. "Hedonism is a mockery of life," I remember her saying. I wrote down that and other things Madou said; in fact, the whole statement was this: "Despair is a waste of life and hedonism is a mockery of it."

Sitting on the dirty stone steps of her saint's church,

Madeleine told me one evening, "One might as well seek protection from a shivering little dog as from a man who manifests his fear of women by trying to dominate them." She flattered me by saying that I was a man to be admired, but, "My father is terrified of passion of any kind, and Clarisse's Randolphe is sucking the life out of my sister with his efforts to secure her as the satisfier of his exhausting needs. He poses as a man, but anyone can see that he is an infant who hasn't had enough of his mother's breast."

I laughed and said, "He is your mother's best hope for a wedding in your household. And isn't he the cousin of a cousin of some marquis?"

"My mother has not given up on you, Philippe," she said.

"Should we consider her proposal?" I asked. "Should we marry, Madou? We are such good friends."

"A good reason not to marry," she proclaimed.

She tapped her chin with her finger, pretending to think seriously about the matter, and then said, "I would marry you, Philippe, if you loved me that way. But you don't, and for good reason. I wouldn't be a good wife."

"And what about your Bohemian friends here?" I asked. "Can't you find a man among them good enough to marry?"

"They celebrate hedonism, not freedom. There's a difference," she said. "And besides, I am more interested in the women like Rosa who are painting, without having to watch themselves socialize in the mirrors of the cafés."

"She is painting cowboys and Indians, isn't she?" I asked.

"I'm not going to tell you. I don't want to be ridiculed," she said. "And I sense you are about to make fun of my adventures." Madou did not like to be made fun of unless she began the joke, nor did she like to be ignored.

3

Rousseau, qui a aimé et a promu l'idée du sauvage noble, etait lui-même un sauvage ignoble.

ROUSSEAU, who loved and promoted the notion of the noble savage, was himself an ignoble savage. He wrote, "Men in a state of nature do not know good and evil." I wonder if he knew the difference himself, since he gave away five infants to the orphanage as soon as his mistress pushed them from her womb. He, like so many philosophers, developed a degree of self-importance and anxiety that today would have been regarded as madness. But his notions live on, encouraging a romantic interpretation of people whose culture is nonetheless decimated. It reminds me somewhat of the scientists who so love a species of bird that they kill the last one to be stuffed and displayed.

At dinner one night in the spring of '88, Madou rushed in very late and began to chatter about Madame Rosa Bonheur's paintings not being very profound, really, but that being with her had given her the opportunity to see noble savages, real indigenous Americans, closely, and to talk with them, and how they were really quite wonderful, and how they were so much more intriguing than the wastrels who hung around the cafés in suicidal intoxication.

"Those poets who write about women as props in their free lifestyles–it's all really nothing more than an infantile indulgence in genital pleasures," she said, dropping her fork rather loudly on the plate. Then, turning to me, she said, "I am so glad you're here tonight, Tic-Toc." I'll admit that her behavior was on the verge of hysteria.

Monsieur Balise threw down his soupspoon, splashing his jacket with a light green cream of asparagus, which I found to be one of the best I had eaten. His eyes were bulging, making me suspect some imbalance of the thyroid, and he said, "I will not have talk about genitals at this table!"

I wondered where he would have talk about genitals, and he continued, saying to his wife in a pleading whine, "These girls, these girls, these monkeys in dresses . . ."

On this night, Clarisse's fiancé of sorts, Randolphe, also known by Madou and me as the Prince of Darkness, was dining with the family, as he did more and more frequently. He seemed suddenly delighted at the way the conversation was going, monkeys and genitalia being two of his favorite topics. He leaned forward and said, dividing his attention between the two other men at the table, me and Monsieur Balise, "There is no woman who is not capable of ruining a man. A Parisian woman is as clever as a monkey but has a better odor."

"The asparagus are so much more tender when they're young," Madame Balise inserted in a large voice.

Madou asked, "Doesn't anyone want to hear about the fantastic things I've seen?" She looked around the table. "I've been intimate with people who live in tribes across the ocean, in the wild mountains of America."

Randolphe patted his mouth and tilted his head. "I want to hear," he said, and I felt that he meant it, for traveling was a passion that cultivated his innocent curiosity and joy. I often wished that Randolphe were traveling.

"There are Americans from the wild places in America, like the ones who were in England for the Queen, you know, last year where Randolphe got his coins."

Indeed Randolphe had gone to the Jubilee celebrations in England and brought back the six penny coins made especially for the occasion as souvenirs for his friends.

"Truly, I have stood right beside them, laughed, even eaten sardines with a group of them right beside a pen where there are bison. Oh, the smell, but they laugh about it, too. Well, they are quite authentic, but intelligent. They make jokes about Europeans." Her eyes were wide. "Rosa knows one who is a chief. The women are so free. They wear such . . . their hair . . ." She moved her hands up to her own head, trying to show the style she had seen. Giving up on that, she dropped her hands back in her lap and said, "The men are quite strong, quite strong, yet without affectation. They actually seem more adult than our men."

Stated innocently enough, this was too blunt and outrageous an insult for Monsieur Balise and Randolphe.

"You are quite silly to suggest . . . ," Balise began.

"Aah," Randolphe chided. "Now we have the truth of it! Madou is lusting for naked savages. So she does have something going on between her thighs!"

"Does anyone want more soup?" Madame Balise sang out.

Madou sat back and sighed. "All your wit is between your thighs, Randolphe. And I am quite tired of it."

"Perhaps you haven't had enough of it," was Randolphe's response. Clarisse sat up straight, as though pinched.

I wanted to put my fist in his mouth.

Madou narrowed her eyes at her father, and there was silence at the table except for his delicate slurping of the soup. "Father, you have nothing to say to this man who violates your daughters?"

"Oh, no more," called out the mother, tilting her head back a little and bringing her hands together to give the picture of a fragile appeal to God.

"Won't you protect us, Father?" Madou said with a mixture of humorous supplication and sad resignation.

Cecile let Pee-Poo lap up some of her soup, which caused Monsieur Balise to swat at the dog, which he missed, knocking Cecile's bowl to the floor. Randolphe applauded casually, like a gentleman at the theater, and said, "Yes, yes! These girls have not had enough discipline. Like monkeys, they're adorable but get out of hand."

Clarisse's head was bowed toward the hands in her lap.

Madou addressed Randolphe: "Are you saying that my sister, whose heart she has entrusted to you, is a monkey? Is this how you indicate your affection for my sister?"

"Your sister's need for affection is insatiable," Randolphe responded. "No man can satisfy it." He patted Clarisse on the head.

Madou rose from the table and said, "You have courted her for four years now without any promise, but with an increased demand on her and this family to feed and entertain you. I have not heard one compliment from your lips regarding her generosity and talents. And the only reason you are allowed at this table is because my mother and father are flattered to be constantly exploited and insulted by diluted royalty."

"Madou!" her mother wailed.

"Has your association with the carousing nephew or cousin or something of a marquis increased your standing at the bank, Father?"

Clarisse now interrupted quietly. "Don't be cruel to Father, Madou."

The two sisters stared at each other as Monsieur Balise cleared his throat. Madou's eyes filled with tears.

I was then in the habit of clinically noting the extreme variations in the tenor of Madou's passion. It changed swiftly, leaving one befuddled, as though one had been eating a piece of chocolate cake and cream, only to have it whisked away and replaced with a steaming plate of onions and fish.

Madame Balise was up and through the kitchen door; Cecile was sitting straight, staring forward, clutching the dog.

"Sit down!" the father yelled at Madou.

The serving girl, Suzanne, followed Madame Balise back into the dining room, ready with rags to clean up the spilled soup. Madou did not sit down but said, "I am leaving for a walk."

Madame Balise implored me to be an escort for her daughter.

I opened my mouth to speak, but Madou's hands, amazingly strong, were pressing down on my shoulders, and she said, "Let him have his lamb, mother."

"I refuse to eat lamb," Cecile said quietly.

The father threw his serviette on the table and stood up.

"What a madhouse!" Randolphe said. "Don't you think they are all mad, Philippe?"

He seemed delighted by the prospect, for it was yet another observation that distracted one from his own chaotic failures. He was somehow independently wealthy and at the same time constantly broke.

I finally spoke up and said, "I can tell you that this is no good for digestion. Perhaps we should all go for a walk and return for the next course."

"Oh, I am mortified," Madame Balise said. "You will never come to dinner again, we have behaved so badly."

"I think he's the smart one," Randolphe said. "Let's go for a walk. Come on, my darling, perfect Clarisse who is so generous and . . . what else was that, Madeleine?"

I stood up and said, "The food is too delicious to forgo, and a bachelor like me is happy to be included even in the unpleasantness of family life from time to time." It may not have been true, but I did indeed feel sympathy and gratitude for the Balise household. "Perhaps I should make some contribution. If it wouldn't bore you, I could tell you about the Austrian couple I met last weekend in Semur-en-Brionnais; they were climbing in the Monts du Charolais."

We moved into the parlor, Madame Balise saying, "Oh, Philippe, you are always such a dear, dear comfort. What would we do without you?"

Randolphe said, "Aah, to be a physician of women!"

Madou kissed my ear and said into it, "I am leaving, Tic-Toc. Eat your lamb and go home to your quiet friends."

She meant my books, my friends. They were always lounging about my apartment in unruly abandon, which my man, Oscar, had given up trying to organize.

"Madou, where are you off to?" her mother asked.

"I am off to the Wild West," she said.

"What does she mean?" Madame Balise asked me. "What did she say? What did she mean?"

I began to distract them by describing the tiled roofs and beautiful gardens of the town where I'd met a couple who had vowed to climb all the mountains in Europe. I was hungry, salivating for a plate of lamb and potatoes, or I would have left with Madou; for when she leaves, it's as though there were ten fewer people in a room. As I spoke of the couple's athletic accomplishments, I was imagining

Madou surrounded by horses and cowboys and bare-chested savages offering her dried buffalo meat. I imagined her learning to ride like a circus woman, standing with one foot on one galloping horse, the other foot on another as she shot at the sky with a gun.

4

Lorsque j'étais en faculté de medicine, j'ai pense un moment étudier le cerveau.

THERE WAS A TIME in my medical training when I considered studying the brain, which was a fashionable passion amongst the scientists at the time. Of course, there was Charcot's influence, which tainted my colleague Tourette, who, if the truth be told, became so singularly focused on the neurological aspects of human behavior that in the opinion of many he was not a competent physician in the general sense, not even capable of recognizing the symptoms of rabies or rheumatism. Although my professional life has recently taken a 180-degree turn, for most of it I chose to be more of a country doctor than an urban scientist. I think for the bachelor such a life is beneficial in keeping up social ties and having some experience of family life. My patients were, I must admit, my family, some playing the part of the distant and fallen cousins and the matronly aunts and doddering uncles. And I had distinct favorites, some for the entertaining aspects of their eccentricities and some for their wisdom and the nobility of their character. Often, my most helpful intervention was simply sitting in a chair by someone's bed and listening to his stories, perhaps leaving bromide or mercury or rheumatic towels to give the impression that some special skill was being applied to his troubles. It was only after the Indian intruded upon my routines that I considered quitting my profession.

One old man, whom I referred to as the Old Soldier, loved to tell stories of campaigns against the Prussians and hunting expeditions in the Loire Valley, where his family owned some crumbling estate. He had a messy combination of gout and rheumatism that would have been alleviated greatly if he did not love pastries and thick gravy so. But it is the rare patient who forgoes pleasure in order to avoid pain. He could forget that pain for a while, when I was sharing a cognac with him and he was telling me for the twentieth time about some barbarism perpetrated by a Prussian officer. I once admitted to being able to speak the German language, which I learned in order to read the markedly superior medical research done in that culture. Rather than infuriating the Old Soldier, my confession prompted his own, which was that in fact he greatly admired the Germans. It is not unusual to find a Frenchman who secretly admires that which he wants to destroy.

For several weeks I was occupied by various of my patients, including the Old Soldier; a few prostitutes, held at the infirmary devised for them at the headquarters of the Paris police; a wealthy bedridden woman, whom I will call the Widow; and a very demanding writer who had several physicians on hand to treat his syphilis, which had advanced into the third stage of painful neurological demise.

In order to securely separate my personal life from my career, I had an office at the Hôtel-Dieu rather than in my own home. My home was and is to me a place in which to allow private habits to flourish without holding them up for public judgment. During my free time, I did not want any company except for my valet, Oscar, and my books and newspapers. I have found that the natural encounters of my profession provided more than enough variety in human experience. And then there were the Tuesday evenings at Charcot's house, where my colleagues met, with the stipulation that no medical talk was allowed. The rule was only loosely followed. The conversations were sometimes about travels some men had made in military service–to places such as Algiers–or about literary scandals.

Often the dinner table was a venue for venting a bleak diagnosis that had been suppressed from the patient. Sometimes there was fierce debate about a new treatment or concerning the diagnosis of a disease. It was at Charcot's table that I insisted on the use of incision to cure emphysema and was told I was a fool. Charcot would have to tap his fork against his wineglass to call our attention back to the purpose of broadening our experiences and having a respite from our professional obsessions. "Gentlemen–the rule!" he repeated, his clean-shaven, round face like a full moon rising at the end of the table.

Sometimes he brought courtesans in to distract us with their stories about the horse races and theater parties. Occasionally a guest was exotic enough to occupy our curiosity, such as the exiled emperor of Brazil, Dom Pedro. I had one good friend at these dinners, Dr. Moulon. He shared my lack of fashion, letting convenience and comfort dictate his wardrobe. And he also knew and in fact was enamored of my Madou.

One night, several weeks after the asparagus-soup event when I had last seen the Balises, Moulon privately expressed a complaint about Madou's lack of interest in him and asked if I had seen her lately. I replied that I had not, and he informed me that she had taken to parting her hair in the middle in an austere betrayal of her lush curls, and she had hemmed her skirts up above her shins. "There's something Siberian in her appearance," he said. He denounced his own compulsions, stating that she really wasn't his sort of woman at all, having a mouth larger than he liked and a refusal to adhere to correct fashion that made her a social risk. I reminded him of his own shortcomings in fashion, which he admitted but claimed were unacceptable in a woman. He confessed that what he liked in her was her healthy constitution and sharp mind. "I could see living with such a woman well, if one didn't feel the urge to control her behavior. But I must confess that I need to exert more influence over my romantic involvements than I guess she would tolerate."

I understood Moulon's attraction and even admired him for his self-reflection, which no doubt kept both him and Madou from a painful attempt at intimacy. Madou was a kind person but somewhat strident about ignoring social trends. It pained her not to be loved, but not as much as it pained her to be enslaved by expectations. My own response to the uncomfortable aspects of social obligation was to seclude myself as much as possible. The Tuesday-night rituals, in which men paraded their wit in the company of those chosen by Charcot for the honor, seemed a necessary balance to my antisocial inclinations. And I had a secret and tentative ambition that required that I understand who was influential in certain areas of my profession.

At some point Tourette, who was one of the medical men at the gatherings who drank too much, made fun of me for using the phrase "in fact" repeatedly. I found that inevitably these evenings ended with some insult, either overt or indirect. More than one of the poets invited never returned, after his talent was given the Latinate name for some disorder. Tourette, his elfin face with its pointed beard, moved from one conversation to another, with a furrowed brow and a smirk on his face. He was in his state of amused study. He often made annoying observations about a person's mannerisms, posture, or pattern of speech. He claimed, after sitting in on the discussion between me and Moulon about Madou, that in his opinion anyone who spoke as bluntly as she was deranged.

I asked, "Are you saying that honesty is a disease?"

He responded, holding the end of his beard, which came to a dark point, no doubt as a result of his pulling on it constantly, "A woman in civilized society who cannot refrain from blurting out her observations is most clearly compulsively dysfunctional."

"In fact," I said, "honesty is an antidote to a most irrational and dysfunctional society."

"Our society?" he shrieked.

"In fact, I am surprised that you who have seen our rampant addictions and syphilitic deterioration and the horrible filth of the poor can consider us civilized!" I was exaggerating my indignation for effect and because of alcohol consumption.

His face was pallid, drained of color except for the beard, which he was grasping as though to pull it from his face. He said, "And you use the phrase 'in fact' with disturbing and pathological frequency!"

"And you are constantly pulling on that beard of yours!"

He dropped his hand and left us.

The day after my conversation with Moulon about Madou, I called upon the Balise family, wanting, in fact, an invitation to dinner. No one was there but Suzanne, the serving girl, whose taciturn demeanor irritated me. But I left my card and was summoned later that day to dine with them the same evening.

Madou greeted me at the door with the new appearance that Moulon had complained about, which I found pure and unaffected. Her hair was tied back with a black ribbon, no false curls or awkward geometries applied. She showed me, by sticking one leg out, her boots, which were made of soft leather and had silver buttons on the sides. The boots, she explained, inspired her to shorten her skirts so that they were more visible. It was never enough for Madou to delight only herself with her adventures.

"I refuse to spend hours in front of the mirror any longer," she said. "What a waste of time. So, if you think I am ugly, don't pity me for it, because I am happy enough."

I laughed, because Madou, in my opinion, could never be ugly. It was assumed that Clarisse was the beauty of the three sisters, but Madou's enthusiastic curiosity and warmth were far more attractive to me than Clarisse's withering moods, made palpable by the presence of Randolphe. That evening the couple was in the bliss of mutual seduction, a mood that made Clarisse's eyes more emerald than usual but that was as impermanent as a plucked tulip. Madou whispered into my ear, "The parlor reeks of courtship tonight." This meant that Randolphe was in his lustful period, a time when he refrained from inappropriate behavior long enough to seduce Clarisse.

"It's good when they are happy with each other," I said.

"Better for the digestion," Madou said.

At dinner, Madame Balise had a placid smile on her face, extolling the virtues of the fish she'd bought for dinner. There was no outburst until Pee-Poo barked and Monsieur Balise said, "For God's sake, for once could we please . . ."

Madame Balise said, "Please do not call out God's name in that way, dear."

Then, whether to turn the tide or because she had

intended to broach the topic with me anyway, Madame said to me, "Philippe, I have a particular request of you."

"Oh, Mother," Madou groaned, apparently knowing what her mother's aim was.

"Madou," Madame Balise continued, "is up to her usual dangerous behavior."

"Dangerous! Oh, how completely ridiculous," Madou called out.

But the mother continued: "Oh, you can see by her look that she has quite rebelled against good taste."

Randolphe spoke up, saying, "Dear doctor, what troubles the poor Madame Balise is that her daughter has become enamored of the bare-chested savages at that American carnival. There's a madness among the women of Paris for these men whose near nakedness is apparently arousing."

"Oh, please, Randolphe," Madou said. "Why must everything have some sordid motivation for you?"

I was beginning to think that the well-cooked lambs and stews of the Balise household could not overwhelm the bitter taste of the chaos at this table.

The mother made a pronouncement: "I think the whole matter should stop. It's a scandal taking these primitives to cafés."

"The lure of the cafés . . . ," Monsieur Balise began, and then shook his head and cut his fish into bite-sized pieces. I noticed him precisely placing a bit of caramelized onion on top of each piece.

"I just . . ." Madame was now affecting a whining

tone, slumping a little so as to exaggerate her need for help in the matter. "Oh, Philippe, will you please escort Madou so at least people will see that she isn't let loose without any decent restraints whatsoever."

Madou jerked up straight in her chair and said to the air above her, "What people, Mother? What people will 'see,' and what are 'decent restraints'?"

"I think I know what 'indecent restraints' are," Randolphe said, laughing and kissing Clarisse on the cheek. She closed her eyes in pleasure.

I wanted dessert, hoping for an egg pudding.

"Randolphe won't go," Madame Balise said with a pout.

"I want nothing to do with that crude circus," he attested. "I find such places horribly boring, truly degrading."

Madou was stuffing bread into her mouth in a comic show of restraining herself from speaking her mind.

Cecile fed Pee-Poo a piece of fish from her father's plate.

Madou swallowed hard, drank some water, and said, calmly, "I am going no matter what. Why don't you come with me, Clarisse?"

The sister said, "No. I'll stay here with Randolphe."

Of course she would, I thought, and I said, "Well, I am insulted, Madou. Why do you so easily dismiss your mother's proposal that I accompany you?"

She looked at me with a gratitude that trapped me completely in the scheme.

"Oh, Tic-Toc, I know how you hate that sort of spectacle. I know how dearly you want your books and coffee at night. But if you would . . . I would love it if you would . . ."

I nodded and she embraced me, tipping her chair to get her arms around my neck like a child after receiving a peppermint candy.

Monsieur Balise said, looking up at his wife at the other end of the table as though just emerging from another world, "Is there any pudding this evening, dear?"

But Madame was not done with her declarations about dangerous behavior.

"I am so glad that Madeleine will have a Frenchman to protect her. Thank you, Philippe, so much."

"Protect me from what? I am the only virgin in the household–well, I'm not sure Cecile counts. Clearly, I have protected myself well enough so far."

Cecile said, "Why don't I count?"

Monsieur Balise banged his fists down on either side of his plate as a kind of bell and said, "We'll have no more talk of virgins at this table!"

"Yes," Randolphe said, unable to hold himself back. "Let's talk about nymphomaniacs!"

Even Madou laughed.

"I see nothing amusing," the father said, "about how this household has completely tumbled into madness! No daughter married. There, I've said it. Not one of my daughters married and . . ." He shook his head, going back to the fish, which had been systematically diminished by Cecile for Pee-Poo's benefit.

Randolphe leaned back in his chair, his hand proprietarily perched on Clarisse's shoulder. Madou stood up and came around behind me and put her arms around my neck.

"Let's go, Tic-Toc. You will see how much more interesting the world is than your routines."

The door to the kitchen swung a little open and Suzanne's head appeared, announcing quietly, "The pudding is burned."

"All right. We're on our way!" I said, standing up. "I'll bring Madou safely home."

"You can spend the night in the parlor if it's late," Madame Balise said.

Suzanne was now collecting plates, and the last words I heard in that household that evening were hers: "There's some cake left from yesterday."

I wondered what kind.

5

Les marchants de journaux dans leurs kiosques, leurs serveurs et les clients dans les cafés, les pigeons, les flâneurs qui regardent les vitrines illuminées des magasins . . .

THE NEWSPAPER SELLERS in their kiosks, the waiters and customers at the cafés, the pigeons, the strollers looking into the illuminated windows of shops, cabdrivers and their horses, the passengers blanketed in the backs of the cabs, all seemed sleepy in the last light of day. But they were not like creatures longing for their beds but like those who are drowsy just after waking. Perhaps the pigeons would retire, but the nighttime engine of Paris was just starting up as we walked along the Rue Royale. Madou asked me which one of the Balise sisters I was most inclined to marry. The joke was aging to the point of having a bad odor.

"Why do you ask such a question? I thought we agreed to protect each other from the vicissitudes of romance." Indeed, we made a litany of asking each other as a greeting, "Are you in love?" as though asking, "Have you succumbed to some disease?"

"You should marry Clarisse," she announced, more giddy than in the apartment. She took deep breaths as though to calm herself. "I hope you like him," she muttered.

"Who?" I asked.

She replied, "My friend. My friend the Indian."

"Ah, yes. It should be interesting," I said.

She raised her eyebrows and sneered, "Yes, interesting."

As on so many evenings that I had learned to avoid, I wanted very much to be going home. I wanted to be sitting in the dark brown leather chair, worn on the right arm, a blanket over my knees as though I were an invalid; reading by the light of dusk coming in through the window, books scattered at my feet; receiving a cup of coffee, heavily creamed, from Oscar. Of course, there were moods to suffer from Oscar. He made it clear, simply by the prim gesture of pushing a book out of his way with the toe of his shoe or by placing my coffee on the arm of the chair with some pains and saying, "It has been scalded a bit," that he wanted for his employer a larger apartment, one with a kitchen and a library, one without the worn leather chair, which he'd happily help the used-items man put in his cart.

But unlike Madou, Oscar did not expect me to be a social pigeon, pecking enthusiastically in tandem at some whim of hers. I quite openly detested other people's whims and could only bear Madou's because of the perfume of her honest character.

"Madou–"

She interrupted, "No, you cannot go home." She grabbed my arm and said, "You are trapped. Oh, Tic-Toc, try to enjoy yourself."

"I'm not in love with Clarisse," I said, to make sure there was nothing I had to pretend to feel.

"All the better. A married couple should not be in love with each other."

I moaned and walked away from her.

"Now you sound like the syphilitic poets of Paris–cynicism mistaken for wisdom."

"Clarisse will marry Randolphe if you don't marry her. You could have such a good life with her–respect and peace. I do not understand her enslavement to that dark beast. You are such a good man, Philippe."

"How do you know, Madou?" I asked. "How do you know I am a good man?"

"I refuse to believe otherwise." She bumped against me.

"I don't think marriage is a healthy state for me," I said.

She agreed, but with the stipulation that perhaps in another landscape, in another climate, marriage would be a different kind of partnership. "There is something sinister about Paris, don't you think?"

"I believe there is something sinister in humans," I responded. "And there are a great many of them in Paris."

"Oh, now you are the cynical one, Tic-Toc. No, I mean how one pretends not to smell the sewers, how those who create beautiful poetry and music and paintings are coughing up blood or addicted to brandy or as mad as feral cats. Even when you look at that pair of lovers cuddling in that cab, there is something sinister, deceitful. I can feel it when I look at my beautiful sister, whose intellectual curiosity seems to have been snuffed out like an altar candle. What happened to her interest in your profession? She's gone mute. Haven't you noticed?"

I shrugged, for though I was more honest with Madou than with anyone else, I would not tell her that a few months earlier I had induced a miscarriage in her sister, a procedure that only Clarisse, Randolphe, and I knew of. It was an episode I detested for several reasons. I would have made confessions to the priests and gone to Mass were I a devout man, free of the limitations reason puts on devotion. I did make a vow to God directly never to provide such a service again, not because I believed I was harming the unborn child, but because I sharply sensed that I was harming the woman, severing a bond more potentially pure, I believe, than any other on earth. It was a procedure among others that added to my questions about my profession and its motives.

"I want to teach my children how to ride horses," Madou announced. "Not around and around a little ring but somewhere where you can go straight for hours at a gallop."

She was quiet, staring at the dark green river but seeing, I was sure, a wide yellow prairie.

"Should we take a cab?" I asked. I saw one available,

the cabdriver just folding up a copy of *Le Figaro* that I might borrow for a glance.

"Oh, come now, Philippe, it is just across the river on the Rue Saint-Dominique. And you who hike up mountainsides like a goat."

I protested that the air was fresher where the goats trod, but she had gone again into some picture of a world that did not include social banter. I worried that she was becoming as intensely sullen as she had been ebullient–a plate of onions and fish; at least one could ignore such a plate more easily than one could ignore chocolate and cream.

The evening was warm and pale now, night unfurling. Even Madou looked languid until she proclaimed, "There it is–see the tents?" as though presenting me with a marvelous gem, when in fact what I saw was a tawdry carnival.

Mexican Joe's Wild West Show was a clump of stained tents on the edge of what was usually grounds for military parades and exercises. A collection of horses, probably purchased from retired Parisian cabdrivers, and a corral with six or seven bison in it provided the rich smell of methane and living animal hides. Such a smell always made me sad, thinking of my mother, whose hands often smelled like the skin of the cows she milked. The grandstands did not quite match up to each other. Like impoverished drunks, they leaned one against the other in front of the battered grounds, where no doubt a number of wars, robberies, and attempted kidnappings had occurred that afternoon.

"There! There!" Madou whispered to me. "There he is."

She was pointing to a group of men standing around a brown horse with a black mane. One of the men was brushing the horse while the others watched and talked to each other, arms crossed over exposed chests. They laughed at some joke, looking down at their feet, and then one, as though sensing attention through his back, turned around and looked at us.

I had, of course, seen pictures of the indigenous Americans, but to see such men walking and talking before me, so casually, did indeed have some thrill to it. I could feel my heart pick up speed. I clung to my perspective as a scholar, trying to note details in a way that might lead to some intriguing anthropological theory to espouse, thus amusing the company at Charcot's. These men were definitely smaller in stature than most of the men I knew. But they had a straightness in posture not at all diluted by the disheveled look of their clothing, for they were in various stages of transition between their show clothes and their pedestrian attire. Shirts were opened; trouser legs were being pulled over boots. One man wore a large hat of feathers, the ubiquitous chief's headdress that fanned out in multicolors around his head and flowed down his back. This array made him seem large, but he, too, was a small man. Their shirts were white or striped and collarless. The men I knew generally wore black clothing in layers that seemed to have little to do with seasons and climate and more to do, I now believe, with hiding something. But these primitives and their Mediterranean complexions gave the impression that they had nothing to hide whatsoever.

Madou said, "Don't they seem bold to you?"

"I was thinking just that," I replied. We were holding ourselves back at a distance so as to make our remarks to each other outside their hearing.

"He is there. That one who is holding the horse's mane now in his fist. That is him–Choice. His name is Choice." And as though he were near enough to hear that he'd just been introduced, he nodded to me, and I nodded back. Madou walked toward him, like an altar boy approaching an altar. I was irritated.

I followed, sauntering irreverently. I was wary and suspicious, wondering if this man had used some means of mental control, some form of hypnotism, to control Madou and contort her will. I took her arm. She snatched it from my grasp and lifted it in greeting to her man. He raised his hand. They then spoke in a code of movements that involved Madou's chin lifting and the man nodding. When I stood before her new friend, he shook my hand, Madou saying in English that I was a doctor. He nodded and smiled. He said in English and French, "Good." There was a Caucasian amongst them, the cowboy of the group. As it turned out, he was from Manchester, England. He knew French, and I asked him how the show had been that afternoon. I was ignoring the Indians' eyes; they all seemed to be studying me, and I felt an infuriating reversal of roles. In fact, I felt self-conscious and awkward, ready to excuse myself and leave Madou to fend for herself and be inducted into their troupe and carted off to Persia.

I had forgotten my question, which the cowboy replied to wit, "The same–horses shitting, guns shooting."

Madou linked arms with her man and leaned her cheek against the hard muscle of his upper arm. Then she broke away, as in obedience to a command, and stood demurely, looking down. I muttered in my head that these men were charlatans and that Madou was under some kind of sinister influence. I would, therefore, accompany them all evening with scrupulous attention to every communication among them. I would gather evidence of my theory and present it to Monsieur Balise. I was then happy to be almost a foot taller than the lot of them.

There is no doubt that jealousy was aroused in me, as well as envy. And I was aroused by the perfection of their bare muscles, though I chastised myself for being as naively passionate as Rousseau about his noble savages and as prone to bias as Thucydides about his beloved Pericles. In fact, there was definitely something of the Greek hero in these men's tautness, akin to the statue of David, whom I imagined looking pensively downward, not demurely but in thought, oblivious to the lesser, clothed individuals who came to study him. In my imagination the statue raised his head and nodded at me. I was startled by this absurd hallucination in my own mind.

Then, as though to wake me from that dream, a few discordant trumpet notes bellowed from a tent on the other side of the complex. Then we heard a drum falling. I exchanged a look of amusement with the Indian named Choice, so as to encourage an intimacy between us that would render him unguarded with me. He nodded at me. The cowboy looking at the dirt he was making into a small hill with his shoe mumbled, "There's the boss."

The gentleman they referred to as Mexican Joe was about one hundred meters away, holding an enormous hat and talking to another of the cowboys just outside one of the tents. Choice said something in his language to another of the Indians in the group, and the two of them laughed. My skin felt very hot, I noticed, and I hoped I wasn't blushing, as my Nordic complexion could go quite crimson. We stood in an awkward clump until the Mexican Joe fellow passed by, giving a taciturn nod and then returning to his thoughts, which seemed to appear on the ground before him.

Madou whispered to me, "He is a deceitful man. He has acted unfairly with Choice. I don't like him."

I decided that I liked this Mexican Joe fellow, who had apparently tamed these savages and had some dominance over them. I imagined myself saying to him, "See here, sir, I am good friends with the Balise family, a family of bankers, and they have entrusted their daughter's care to me since she was a girl." Then I would warn him in a gentlemanly way to keep his showmen from taking advantage of her enthusiastic and generous spirit.

I strolled toward the bison and passed the Mexican Joe fellow again, who was scratching his head and calculating to himself as all businessmen do. At the last possible moment he looked up to see me and gave me the kind of smile people put on their faces so as to say, "I am not your enemy but I'm not particularly interested in being your friend either." I saw, at close range, that his face was mottled with purple veins, the clear sign of alcohol addiction. I pretended interest in the bison.

When the showmen were fixed in their evening attire, they were closer to the European style, disguised somewhat with black coats. I stared at Choice, telling myself I was doing so for Madou's sake, but finding my mind lost in an admiration of his deportment; I would call it stoic, especially in light of the torment he was suffering internally, which manifested itself later as a deadly illness. He did not demonstrate a need to ingratiate himself to others with chatter. In fact, I felt uncomfortably foppish in comparison, to the point of wanting to reveal some flaw in him, especially to Madou. My height and blond complexion, so often complimented as handsomely robust, began to feel lumbering and pale. I suddenly wondered if I did not like to socialize not because of my disdain for others but because of some buried disdain for myself. This was the kind of self-reflection that this primitive induced in me, without speaking a word, and I was quite confused by it and still am.

When it was dark enough so that a few stars were visible in the sky, five of us, Choice and another Indian, the cowboy from Manchester, I and Madou, passed underneath the banner over the entrance to the carnival.

Choice wore a top hat very much like my own, except that two braids came from beneath it. We were a moving Tower of Babel: Madou knew a few words of the Indians' language and was fluent in English; I could speak fluent German, especially when the topic was infectious diseases and neurological lesions; the other Indian with the flowing hair and no hat spoke his own language, some French, and a little English; the cowboy spoke English and French; Choice spoke mainly in his own language when he did speak, which was infrequently. But I sensed, especially after I got to know the man better, that he understood much more than others assumed. Choice, I believe, was fond of letting other people make ignorant assumptions; it amused him and allowed him to observe without having to participate. I understood this well.

Madou led us to the Café du Palais, an uncrowded place where there were mainly government workers and university students wanting a simple glass of wine and a stew.

"You can get your egg pudding here," she said to me. And this did cheer me up, a consolation for suddenly feeling like an eel amongst trout.

The patrons of the café, including a wife here and a sister there, marveled openly at the spectacle of the indigenous men. And Madou's defiantly drab colors and riding skirt didn't conform well to this middle-class clientele. The stout waiter with a bulbous nose indicated a somewhat insulting amusement at the party we all made. The Indians themselves behaved with thorough familiarity with everything but the language. They had been in Europe, it turned out, for more than a year. The rotund little server pretended not to understand the one Indian's French, which was clear enough to me. But even insults seemed to be funny to Choice and his comrade. Madou was smiling and reached out and held her man's wrist. He patted the side of her hand; I noted that he seemed fatherly toward her, though he was not much older than she.

Choice was the least talkative of our party, and yet I constantly felt that he was more present than anyone. This was only one of the confusing impressions I had. At this time in my life, perhaps less so than when I was a student, I greatly disliked being confused, especially by my own emotions. I wanted simplicity and order. Madou whispered to me that Choice liked me. And whenever I looked at him, his eyes were already on me and he nodded and smiled. Madou was sitting straight, mostly looking at the space in front of her, at nothing in particular. She could have been mistaken for someone on morphine were her posture not so stiff. Occasionally, she leaned toward me and said something softly, such as, "He and his friend were left behind by another show, that performed for Queen Victoria's Jubilee." She pulled herself back up and in a few minutes bent toward me again and added, "He's been to Mount Vesuvius and Germany."

The cowboy from Manchester was pontificating loudly about what a rogue this Mexican Joe fellow was, paying one dollar a day, which was more than the other fellow paid, but one had to buy one's own food, for the most part, so it was impossible to save a dime.

Choice listened, his back so straight that his upper torso seemed to be leaning back a bit. He was perhaps ten years younger than I and barely taller than Madou. His lips were full and curved below a rather prominent nose. He had close-set eyes, almost seeming crossed at times. I was grateful that he had taken off his hat and hung it on one of the hooks in the column beside our table. By wearing it, he seemed to make fun of me and my whole society. He clearly had a mischievous humor evident in his expressions and gestures.

He spoke to his friend with the free-flowing hair, who then spoke to the cowboy, who then said to me, "Choice here would like to know if you are, as his lady friend has told him, a man of medicine."

I looked at the source of the inquiry, whose face suddenly looked as old as my grandfather's, and I said, "Yes," thinking that he meant to ask my help on some pain or affliction he was suffering. But instead he put his hand on his chest, his fingers splayed, and nodded once.

"He's supposed to be a healer among his people–a medicine man," the cowboy from Manchester said.

"What do you mean 'supposed to be'?" I asked.

Madou answered. "He is not fully trained yet. That's part of why he wants to return so badly. He says his people need him there to heal them."

"What's wrong with his people?" I asked. There was a bitter, scornful edge to my voice.

Choice said something to his friend, who then said in broken French, so that I wondered if the words were correct, "The sickness is the white man." And then Choice kindly said to me, "Not all."

An uncomfortable cacophony of thoughts went through my mind, including the scoffing opinions that my colleagues and teachers would have of whatever primitive and superstitious healing this Indian was referring to. My neck grew hot, and I discovered that my eyes and his were locked, neither one of us looking away until he nodded and put out his hand for me to shake.

Madou transferred the tensions of our table onto the waiter, yelling out at him to bring the coffees and pudding before she went into the kitchen herself. I was happy to see her able to reanimate herself as needed. My hand, feeling obscenely soft, was still in Choice's. He smiled and let go, looking again simply like a young man traveling the world. Madou demanded bread and cheese from the server. I ordered a cognac, and Choice said no other word. Instead Madou quietly told me that he was concerned for his health, that he was feeling weak and in fact had been diminishing in strength since he left the harbor of New York almost two years earlier. He had signed up with his friends, young adventurous men, to see the world. He wanted to study the culture of whites, who seemed destined to take over his homeland. He wanted to travel to the places where white men got their impressive power; he wanted to see the place where Jesus had died and become a god. But as what he called the fireboat furrowed the waters past the huge Statue of Liberty outside New York City, the hold full of braying and moaning animals, Choice had felt the first of his illness, a sickening dread that he would never come back to his place, to his way of life. And now, Madou explained, the sickness was worse. He seemed healthier than any man I had ever seen.

"What are his symptoms?" I asked.

Madou knew the answer and said, "Oh, there are things he has seen, powerful images that drain his strength."

I was excitedly composing this aspect of the story for the Tuesday-evening men, who had a passion for the demented psyche. I said, "What sorts of images can make a man physically ill?" I told the statue of David in my mind to keep quiet.

"Many of his people starved, you see"–Madou's eyes were filling with tears, and I looked angrily at them and listened as she continued–"one winter when he was a boy–and a very great man named Crazy Horse was killed when he was a boy . . . He says that he feels the injustice of it like . . . like poison someone has poured into his ear. And he keeps seeing the beautiful stallions that died on the ship that went across the ocean, their sleek carcasses tossed into the water, disappearing behind him in the sea, which was so much more vast than he had been able to imagine. These are his symptoms."

The cowboy from Manchester yawned musically and the Indians stretched. The table was a clutter of the remnants of our little meal. The waiter was leaning against the door looking outside. Two lovers had come into the café, which inspired Madou to straighten up and sit with more distance between her and Choice. I felt that she wanted to protect his dignity, to ensure that he would not be seen as just another man in Paris, courting a woman in some café.

The cowboy remarked that the thing he hated most about wars was the death of animals.

I was pressed by Choice's Indian companion to describe the war with Prussia, which I had no recollection of, since I was a boy in 1870, living on a farm near Rouen. But I knew well enough the stories of my patients, including the Old Soldier, who admitted to me once that he was awakened sometimes in the night by the screams of a young man he'd fought with who'd had his leg ripped off by a canon blast coming from his own ranks. I tried to discuss the bravery of the Frenchmen and the patriotic nobility of our cause, but I kept returning to some graphic description of battlefield surgeries I had heard about from my teachers. I ordered another cognac and stumbled to explain the reasons for the war, the dispute over territory, the various injuries to the French. I lost track of my own point and was glad when the Indian with the long, untethered hair spoke brokenly about the show's depiction of Indian wars, and how Custer was like Napoléon, only more insane. I needed an explanation of who Custer was, and the Englishman from Manchester said, "Just don't ask about Crazy Horse, or we'll be here until dawn." He yawned again. I guessed that Crazy Horse was Choice's Pericles.

At some point I asked the Englishman how he had come to join the show, and he said that it was mainly to infuriate his father, a British solicitor who'd managed to scare off a sporting girl who might have been his wife had she had a better last name. He said it was a long story and saddened him, so he stood up to leave.

Nodding toward Choice, he said, "You know, I met him in Sheffield, where I'd fled to elope with my girlfriend. But she never arrived for some reason I'll never know. I met up with Choice and his friend, who'd been quite stranded."

Choice looked straight ahead, but his lips moved, making words in what language I didn't know.

"Buffalo Bill," the cowboy said, "the great Mr. Cody, had sailed back to America, leaving two of his men quite behind, just as my dear girl did me. There were the three of us, having missed the boat entirely–a pathetic gang of lost boys, I'd say!"

Choice slowly raised his hand up, cautioning the man.

"He doesn't want me to say anything rough about his man," the cowboy said. "Indeed, there was no malicious intent. Certainly Mr. Cody is a gentleman, not like our Mexican Joe. Old Joe popped up like a jack-in-the-box with a sombrero on, whiskey breath and all, promising all kinds of things. And I signed on, too, though I had a hell of a time learning to trot a horse without bobbing up and down. Ha! What a talker that Mexican Joe is!"

As the cowboy was standing, telling his account, a conversation about Boulanger grew loud at the next table, where two men were drinking Tokay. One fellow insisted that General Boulanger's desire to reinstate a monarchy was enlightened, and the other was just shaking his head no and inserting one or two words. They got loud enough to be a spectacle, and we were quiet. Choice put his fist to his mouth, quickly opening it up and away from his lips over and over again, and said, "Words. Too many words."

He now looked ill, as though the symbolic vomiting of his gesture had drained him. Madou was practically sleeping on his shoulder. Gently moving her, Choice stood up, his lips trembling. He stumbled outside, though I knew that he had not had a sip of alcohol. I followed quickly, engaging my duties as a doctor with the comfortable firmness of a race horse who hears the gun. The Indian was leaning against the wall of the café in the shadows, away from the streetlight. His head was hanging and shaking, and I had the impression that he had in fact just vomited.

Madou was behind me asking if he was all right.

I put my hand on his shoulder, which seemed absurdly massive underneath the black jacket and white shirt. Choice suddenly pushed himself away from the wall, turned, and shook my hand with comic vigor. He then placed his hand over his stomach and said, "Ate too much white man." Then he grabbed me by the shoulders, kissed the air beside both of my cheeks, and said, "You and me–healers, friends." And again he shook my hand, mocking the American habit with exaggerated fervor. He laughed.

I didn't see him for a long time, although I believe that from that night on I dreamed his dreams from time to time. Some of my colleagues had some interest in how dreams reveal one's psychic abnormality. I did not reveal the odd changes in the images and textures of my dreams to the esteemed neurologists at Charcot's Tuesday evening. I simply stated one evening, before doing my part with the violin to accompany a Chopin étude for piano, that I did not think that one could find a man's dreams in the tissues of his brains.

6

Que penses-tu de lui?

"WHAT DO YOU THINK OF HIM?" Madou asked me as soon as we were alone and walking across the Pont de la Concorde.

Having had three cognacs, I did not have my usual ability to analyze and therefore circumvent a nagging peevishness. Perhaps I would have recognized jealousy or fatigue or even intoxication as causes for what I blamed Madou for–an irritation with the world. In fact, I believe now, having scrutinized my behavior during these times so as to understand the changes I and the Balise household went through, that I was becoming thoroughly irritated not with the world but with myself. There is some catalyst in what we imagine a quiet stranger sees in us that makes us uncomfortably aware of things we have avoided.

But I answered Madou with a mean-spirited quip: "I think you are romancing a fantasy, Madou, some idea of the noble savage because of your own boredom and lack of purpose in life."

She walked silently beside me for several minutes and then said, "How cruel you can be, Philippe, and I never knew it." I felt bestial, and yet all I could do was stop at a kiosk and buy a newspaper, one I had never bought before: *l'Humanité.* Tucking it under my arm, I commented, "Perhaps I should become more humane." She did not so much as smile at my joke. So I added, "I am only trying to protect you, Madou."

She replied, "Thank you so much, my dear Dr. Normand, for counting yourself amongst the numbers of men who want only to protect us women. I still have not deciphered from what it is you want to protect us, if not yourselves."

It was the first time harsh words had passed between us without a mollifying smile, and I felt an urge to abuse her more, to expose her as a twittering sparrow who flew from one interest to another, causing twigs to dance in the wind. At least I had enough sobriety to see my own wickedness and clamp my mouth shut.

"You are going in the wrong direction," she announced, and then quickly kissed my cheek and strolled off toward her house. I thought of following, just to see her safely home before taking a cab to my own apartment, but as I watched her formidable gait, back straight, I was certain that only a fool would try to molest her and believe he would not himself suffer the greater injury.

When I arrived home, Oscar was more peevish than I when he saw which paper I carried. I tossed it in a chair and said, "I hardly noticed which paper I was buying, and besides you cannot believe that I would be vulnerable to socialist propaganda."

He shrugged, as though it were none of his concern.

That night I dreamed of beautiful horses being tossed into the ocean and drowning. I awoke after seeing myself ask the Indian healer if I could smell his skin. I felt a bit underwater myself when I walked into the front room, where my coffee was sitting, as usual, on the table. Beside it, Oscar had carefully placed *l'Humanité* and a note from the syphilitic writer requesting that I come around and bring some ether.

"Ether!" I grumbled, and opened the paper, snapping it loudly for Oscar to hear.

I saw Madou a few weeks later, carrying paints and holding a sun hat under one arm, something one might see in the south on a farm girl. She gave me a large smile and trotted to greet me, the paint box rattling under her arm.

"Oh, Tic-Toc, I haven't seen you for so long!" There were freckles on her nose, which I kissed, and she said, "So, you are not angry with me."

"What are you up to?" I asked her, pinching her chin a little.

"You with your brilliant scientific mind should be able to figure that out."

"Painting, I see. So, you are no longer the mascot of painters, but one yourself."

She studied me: "Are you being cruel again? Now I don't trust you."

"No, no, no. Madou, really, I am just teasing and glad

you are being bolder with your own talents. Soon I will find you in an absinthe stupor at the du Tambourin."

"You cannot stop teasing!" she said, laughing. "What has come over you?"

People were passing us, annoyed with the impediment we presented. A man walking his bicycle seemed to be aiming right for me.

"Let me walk you to the quay, if that's where you're going. I'm weary to the bone of my spoiled patients. I feel that I am doing nothing of importance." My statement seemed melodramatic to my own ears, so I quickly said, "How is your man?"

"Oh, he left a few days ago, to Germany."

"Aah," was all I could say.

She said, "We had such fun. Choice and his friend wrote down words for me to learn in their language. He said when he came through again he would see how well I'd done with them. It's nothing like French or English or even German. Rosa and her friends call me the Indian's lover."

"You are happy, Madou, not like most women whose lovers have gone away."

Showing me her disapproving face, she stopped to put the paints down for a moment and smash the hat on her head, putting her eyes in shadow so that they were open more widely now, lighter than usual, more green than brown. "Why do you presume that he is my lover? You know, people presume that you and I are lovers. Why must every man and woman who walk down the street be undressed and copulating in the minds of others? You sound like Randolphe, always assuming that people are copulating. Now that he's aware of the lesbians, he'll even say it about two women."

"I'm happy to see you," I told her.

"Pee-Poo and the Prince of Darkness miss you."

"That would be a good novel or play, wouldn't it? *Pee-Poo and the Prince of Darkness*."

"Come around soon," she said. "I'm painting everyone's portrait and I'll do yours."

"So, are you in love, Madou?"

She laughed and said, "No. Are you?"

And I said, "No."

We shook hands like two comedians congratulating themselves on surviving a kick to the buttocks.

"Good!" she said. "It's you and I against the world of fools, then!"

When I strolled away, I was in a far better mood than I had been since the night I sat with her and her friend. I suddenly had the desire to buy a newspaper and sit at a café near the opera house, where none of my patients were likely to see me.

7

Plus d'un mois passa avant que je rencontra Madou et sa famille de nouveau.

Over a month passed before I again saw Madou and her family. Several emergencies had presented themselves to me, including a horrible accident in the fourteenth arrondissement in a sordid area between the railway and the fortified wall. A railroad worker had his right leg crushed by a railway car that toppled over during some misguided attempt to raise one side of it for repairs. Normally, I would not have been involved in this tragedy, but I was summoned to attend to him by a friend of his, one of the prostitutes I'd seen in the jail. She had bad teeth from constantly smoking, and from that I recognized her immediately when she met me in the street and pleaded, pressing a few damp sous into my hand, that I go see her friend, who had been injured that morning. I returned her coins but decided to go see what I could do for the man.

I am not unfamiliar with the part of town near the railroad that circles Paris like a giant toy. And I am not so terrified of the stories of crime and violence there as some who discuss such matters as though their own lives were at risk, as they sit in front of plates full of food in some velvet parlor. As I have an office in the Hôtel-Dieu and work in the jail from time to time, I understand the circumstances of the laboring classes, who cannot afford to hide their immorality as well as the rich do. I am no Guesdist, though Oscar suspected so, since I was more often bringing home newspapers with a Marxist lilt, but my experiences and observations were beginning to inform me of the equality of the classes when it came to immorality. And now I am certain that the more leisure a man has, the more mischief he indulges in; whereas the more leisure a woman has, the more priests she consults. I cannot say why one gender prefers to indulge its boredom with hedonism and the other with spirituality, but I can say that whereas I have more respect for the latter, I enjoy the stories of the former more. There is nothing more tedious than a pious woman, though she is probably less likely to cause mental and physical injury than the man who feels entitled to take what he wants in the material realm. The mass result of such greed is an economy so skewed as to topple the world. But these words come now. When I was attending the poor railroad worker, I believed, like so many of my colleagues, that even poverty was an inherited trait, not unlike the ideas of the Hindus regarding classes of men. I believed that my duty was simply to dispense kindness and skill without going so far as to jeopardize my own position. I was willing to administer to the poor only to the extent that I could afford. Perhaps they do better to avoid physicians; I have more and more come to believe that we are mostly charlatans, used to feed and in some cases even create addictions, paid to alleviate fears.

The injured man was in a delirium when I went to his home. It was a clean but small two-room affair, which he shared with his very petite wife and three children. The youngest child was an infant, whose lethargic demeanor marked it for the grave. I had always avoided children as patients, for a number of reasons. The medical profession, which is willing to create torment in a human in order to rescue him from death, does not accommodate the pure intuition of children not to have their pain increased. I cannot, therefore, argue with a child who screams not to have his already broken arm painfully manipulated. Shamefully I had to admit to my colleagues, who laughed at my unwillingness to treat children, that in the face of their suffering, reason was not as strong in me as pity.

The laborer's delirium was a kind of anesthesia against the horrible condition in which he found himself. There was nothing left of his lower right leg recognizable as a human limb. I had to tell the wife, who smelled of sour milk and sweat and who spoke with her knuckles pressed against her teeth, that I must remove the leg from above the knee. I did not tell her that I had failed to contrive the facts so that I could minimize the removal, cutting below the knee. A leg that is amputated above the knee impairs one's balance significantly more than a leg ending just below the knee. But it is tragedy enough for the uneducated household, where I was now a god, to say that their man's leg would be thrown in a cesspool. When the wife cried out, it was to say, "He'll not be able to work!" I responded, "He'll not be able to live if I do not remove that limb."

With children crying, neighbors coming in and out, and the wife silently acting as assistant, I did my duty. We placed the man on the table, and then I distanced myself from the task, letting my hands think for me. I imagined to myself a passage of music from a Bach cello sonata, for I liked its circuitous logic. I repeated the tune over and over in my head until I was in a kind of mesmerization. My concentration thus focused, my actions became automated and as precise as I was capable of. I was able to say to his wife, as though instructing her about the preparation of bread, "Lay on his chest to keep him still." My steady hand poured carbolic acid on his wounds, and when his writhing was done, I proceeded to cut with the surgical saw so familiar to the laborer and the soldier while mostly unknown to the wealthy and the generals; they deftly avoid the maiming tasks they put into motion. All the while, I was repeating the same tune over and over to myself, and an observation came into my head in the voice of the Indian man, which said that I owed as much to my familiarity with music as to my familiarity with science. Such was the distraction my automatic mind put between me and my patient's trauma. The man's defense was to lose consciousness, his thin wet hair pasted against his shining skull, so the carbolic acid and boiled rags applied to his newly crafted stump did not agitate him.

When I stood away from my work and helped to lay the man back on his bloody cot, I was surprised to note the silence of the household. The children were asleep, the light outside much dimmer than when I had begun, and the wife was preparing a stew on the hearth, which could just as well have been in a Neanderthal's cave. Quietly, she said to me, "Let me give you something to eat before you leave, doctor."

I shook my head, too exhausted to speak. I left as many francs as I had in my pockets on a stool beside the cot. The wife pretended not to see, and I took up the bucket full of the filth I had removed from the man, the tissue that used to be his foot, ankle, shin, and knee, and the rags that had caught his blood, and I left.

I threw all of this behind old train cars, into a cesspool in a disheveled field. I then reentered my life by way of a café halfway between that place and my own apartment. As I sat staring at a newspaper account of a soldier's experiences in Algiers that seemed incomprehensible to me, I realized that I had not told the woman how to dress her husband's injury. A bleak resignation then overtook me, and I knew that in a few weeks, at most, the man and the infant would be dead. I thought bitterly that a primitive medicine man could have done as well, rattling bones and chanting nonsense. And I wondered if primitive men experienced the same dizzying contrast between one class and another. Where there were no parlors and no factories, I supposed there was not the same disparity between the opulent and the miserable. And yet, I thought, in perfect keeping with the logic of my culture, was it not better to have the potential to acquire luxury than to guarantee the comfort of all? Equality, as de Tocqueville has noted, can result in a deadening mediocrity, a dull and unprogressive society of bumpkins. But there seemed to be something brutally stubborn in using one's intelligence to manufacture profit but not to obliterate poverty.

When I crossed the Avenue Breteuil, I had returned to humming that same passage from the Bach sonata that I had put in my mind while amputating the poor man's leg.

The very next afternoon, I was walking along the Quai des Tuileries and saw Madou riding a bicycle. Her wide grin made my own mouth turn upward, and she stopped with both grace and strength, as though she'd ridden the contraption since birth. She was an entirely engaging combination of manliness and femininity, her strong legs in riding bloomers splayed out on either side of the bicycle and her sweet curls, so simply tied back, blowing in the river's breeze.

"Are you in love?" she asked first.

I shook my head and found, horribly, that tears were filling my eyes. Madou let the bicycle drop and grabbed my forearm with both her hands.

"Oh, Philippe, what can have happened?"

I shook my head, smiling, shrugging, unable to speak,

the tears brimming over, and I could only utter, "I'm sorry. Please forgive me, Madou."

"I'll forgive you if you tell me what has happened."

I shrugged again. "Nothing. Nothing has happened. Really. An attack of nerves. Nothing."

The uncomfortable melancholy was over, and I breathed deeply. Madou's dark, heavy eyebrows were furrowed and she was not smiling, but I was.

"Don't worry. Just forgive me. You look like an Englishwoman on that bicycle."

"Oh, not so drab as that!" Madou sneered.

"Queen Victoria herself."

"I'll have to stuff my bosom for that."

"Well, then I will be in love," I said.

"So that's the secret to your heart–a large bosom. I had no idea."

"I have been bad not to come around."

"Then stop being bad. Come to dinner tonight and I can show you my paintings."

She took my hand and I pressed hers. Seeing a streak of green paint on her finger, I felt, again, like weeping, and determined that I would medicate myself with a glass of cognac.

"I'll walk with you awhile," she said.

"No, no. I have to go see the writer. He's dispensing strawberries dipped in ether, and it's all a ridiculous mess. The poor man has gone partially blind in one eye now. But I'll come around for dinner later."

She left, riding the bicycle, weaving through a sparse stream of walkers.

Dinner at the Balise household was unremarkable in that the conditions were the same, perhaps a little advanced. Pee-Poo's viscous eye drainage was damper and darker, and I did not like looking at his head lolling over Cecile's plate. Clarisse was not at the table, and Monsieur Balise was threatening to put her in Salpêtrière because she alternated between hysterical fits and morose confinements to her bed. Her condition was intimately connected with Randolphe, of course. Almost two months ago, she had fought with him, finally telling him that she could not endure his emotional bondage any longer in that the coldness he punished her with came in larger doses than his affection. This, according to Madou, who told me the story in the closet that operated as her painter's studio, was a moment of sanity on Clarisse's part. But in the weeks in which they were separated, Clarisse weakened at the sight of herself without a lover and so got involved with a man she met at the theater. In the swift and dramatic courting stage, this gentleman wrote her love letters that pronounced precisely what she needed to hear: that she deserved nothing but kindness; that she would be a wonderful mother to the children of some lucky man; that her talents, including her intellectual abilities, combined to create in her an admirable companion; that she had awakened in him an admiration that would lead inevitably to a passionate serenity and lifetime devotion. She had a sexual liaison with the man and immediately regretted it.

The truth, as Madou saw it, was that he was incompetent as a lover. His words were a lie, promising affection that he could not otherwise give. His most impassioned act was to vow to kill Randolphe for all his insults to Clarisse. Clarisse fell into a horror of what she had done, what she had lost in the intimate comfort of having Randolphe as a lover and adjunct to her family. She wailed that she could not be alone, that she had made an enormous mistake and needed Randolphe. So distraught was she that Monsieur Balise demanded that she be taken to Salpêtrière and treated there for hysteria. It was the mother who went to fetch Randolphe. He came nobly, giving Clarisse a morally superior shoulder to weep on. But in the weeks that followed, he had seemed to exhibit a new entitlement for demeaning Clarisse. Madou shook her head and groaned, describing the new weapons he had to make her endure his cold shaming. That very evening he had raged against her for destroying the other man's letters, which she had promised to let him read. He had wanted to examine them thoroughly himself. Madame Balise begged Randolphe to forgive her daughter, to see that her daughter was sick with shame, but he left angrily, and Clarisse went back to bed.

"Clarisse has torn apart her room looking for those letters, and I had to tell her that I took them myself. I took them and threw them into the river. I think she will never speak to me again."

"Why?" I asked. "Why did you involve yourself in their destructive dramas?"

Madou shook her head again.

"I cannot stand another increase in his ability to crush my sister's energy. I cannot stand any other excuse for him to reduce her to his heartless control, to the cold liberties he takes with my sister's spirit."

"Was there something in the letters . . . ?"

"Only phrases he could taunt her with, shame her with, her own weakness displayed in the conversations the letters referred to in which my sister spoke of joy she had not felt in months, of her desire to have a child with a man who loved her. He promised that he would never make her kill her own child. An odd statement to say the least! I felt that such dramatic statements would simply increase Randolphe's mania."

I recalled Clarisse's miscarriage and my part in it. I recalled Randolphe weeping and asking me to be sure that Clarisse suffer no pain. There was some hint of his adoration of Madou's sister, but I could not tell her of the incident; I could not tell her why I believed that what Randolphe hated more than Clarisse herself was his attachment to Clarisse.

From a painting behind Madou, the swirling head of her exotic friend Choice watched us. There were several portraits, uniquely disturbing, that inspired a great deal of thought. I was drawn in by vibrant colors in little slashes that made the faces seem to tremble, and I was sad to say that I saw a glaring lack of talent in her efforts. It was here that I finally glimpsed the wall around our friendship's honesty.

"How did you do this, Madou? Where on earth did you get a notion to use such a style?"

"I don't know," she said.

The portrait of Clarisse's face was dominated by a sickly combination of green with red shadows. Her skull seemed about to implode, already caved in on one side owing to what lapse in artistic perspective I could not say.

Another face, of a bearded poster artist, at least captured well his maniacal ugliness.

I had to look away again and finally wanted to leave the room.

"Have you shown your work to your friend Madame Bonheur or any of the others?"

"Oh, no," Madou said. "I haven't had any formal instruction, you know. No, I am just experimenting on my own. Just amusing myself."

She stared affectionately at the Indian's face, saying, "Yes, I suppose it would be nice if someone noticed and thought them good. Father thinks them a waste of time. He is encouraging me to take on students, to tutor his employer's two children in English."

The little exposition of her work made me quite sad. I was sad for Madeleine's lack of promise and for the dishonesty that was now between us. I could not say to her, "These are hopelessly unskilled, my friend." I wanted to throw them all in the Seine to float along with Clarisse's letters, so that the whole river would be full of the drifting remains of the Balise household's misguided whims.

When Madou turned to me, I touched her cheek, and she said, "Let's go to the gardens." I could say nothing and was grateful that she did not ask my opinion of her work.

It was fall and the Tuileries were more barren than ever. After we walked almost half the length of the gardens, Madou lay on her back among some shrubs, her arms bent behind her head, her eyes closed. I stood above her and dropped crumbled dry leaves on her face. There was some light from the gas lamps and a half-moon that was blurred by mist. Without opening her eyes Madou smiled and said, "Oh, doctor, doctor, what medicine do you have for me?"

"What ails you?" I asked.

"Loneliness," she said. "I am lonely and I'm not even sure for what."

I sat down on the ground, holding my knees. "Perhaps you are in love, Madou, and are lonely for your man, Choice. But I worry that you have made him into a sort of myth, a fantasy."

"I don't belong here on my own," Madou told me. "Have you noticed that there is a tacit presumption that a woman's freedom is defined by her promiscuity? To be free as a man is to say and create and do as one wants. To be free as a woman is to be available to a man when he wants her. It is too confining, too demeaning for me. At least when Choice was here, I felt . . . hopeful about the world, about myself, I should say. I felt protected. You know, Tic-Toc, my sexual urges are definitely linked with a feeling of being protected. I am overwhelmed with desire when I feel a man is capable of protecting me as he would a daughter, with prejudice toward me and my capabilities, with a desire to present me to the world as strong and good. It is quite an intoxicating aphrodisiac."

I had to laugh and say, "But how you mock the idea of being protected by anyone!"

She sat up. "You're not listening. I said that he protects me as though I were his eldest daughter, as though I were something important, intimately important to him and worthy of admiration and affection."

"Will you see him again?" I asked.

"Oh, yes. He said he would see me when he is in Paris again. But he is most determined to go back to America. He feels shame that he is not there. He said that as a doctor you would understand the shame of having skills to alleviate suffering and not being able to use them."

I thought of my writer patient, who, in his deluded state, was insisting upon mercury treatments, which his disease was far too advanced to warrant. The medicine itself would have had a worse effect on him than his disease, especially mixed as it would be with his ether and wine habits.

"I wish I had the same confidence in my skills," I said. "In fact, Madou, I often believe that nature and time are more successful at resolving illnesses than doctors are. I admit that sometimes the resolution is the relieving benevolence of death." My writer patient, for all his blithe writing about human tragedy, was terrified of death. He blamed women for it. And he hated them for debauching men and making pets of them. He was on my mind because he had called for me every day for four days. I knew that there would be a message from him when I returned home.

I stood up and held out my hand. "Let me walk you back home, Madou. This talk of my profession has made me feel melancholy."

She said, "Why, Tic-Toc, how odd to hear you say such a thing. You are a fine doctor."

"Come on then. Let me walk you home," I said. My hand was still held out in the air above her.

"I'm staying," she said.

"You'll catch cold lying on the ground, Madou."

She shrugged.

"All right then," I said, and I left.

I was indeed called in the middle of the night to the syphilitic writer's home. He was suffering a bad spell. A woman he'd hired for dictation had become an avid attendant, disgusted by the chaos of the household as she had found it. She had, in fact, moved in and was copying manuscripts, organizing bits of stories, transporting work to newspaper offices. The writer, she admitted coolly, was often abusive with words, ranting and confused. She warned me against mentioning anything to do with removal to any kind of institution. His diseased and creative mind would not stop, like a perpetual-motion machine or some malevolent toy. I sat beside his bed, watching his jaw tighten and loosen, listening to his heart through the stethoscope, though to what purpose other than to prove that I was a physician I cannot say. I heard his voice through the tubes, coming as though from a cave where his soul huddled: "All women are whores" and "Deceit is the foundation of marriage." These were the kinds of thoughts he sucked on.

"Why does my hair fall out?" he asked petulantly.

I answered, "It is the disease, man. You have a disease and that is one of its symptoms."

In the hallway, I conferred with his secretary, whose slim olive face showed determination without sentimentality.

I told her, "The best thing you can do for him is to incite his philosophical convictions. They distract him. Other than the basics required for his survival, I encourage you to provide stimulation for his opinions, for I noted that his muscles relaxed as he was complaining about the world in general as opposed to himself in particular."

She nodded. I expected her to snap her heels together. When I saw a spiked Prussian helmet in the hallway hanging with the other hats, I easily imagined it on the small head of the formidable secretary.

No mention was made by me, the writer, or any of his acquaintances, including my much-esteemed colleague Dr. Tourette, who considered himself a literary man, of the method by which my patient acquired his fatal and demeaning affliction. Most believe that the chancres and rashes that eventually transform into paralysis and madness are transmitted by a combination of inheritance and contagion. I have seen the progression of this disease and am certain, though not willing to argue the point, that it is transmitted solely by contagion, through the entrance to a woman's womb, either to the baby who passes through it or to the man who uses it for his pleasure. Paris is proud of its immorality, though, and does not easily accept the direct relationship between that immorality and its diseases, wanting no impingement on its version of freedom. But, like Madou, I see no freedom inherent in bondage to pleasure, a bondage that is addiction in many cases. Neither do I see freedom in the eyes of the hungry bastards created by a society unwilling to look more deeply for its liberation than to what is between their legs. This was all taking on sinister tones in the context of the news from London of a man who was going about killing women with surgical precision: prostitutes, in fact, were his victims. Meanwhile, Oscar was muttering again about the humiliation and inconvenience of our living quarters, wanting to move to a larger set of rooms and hire a cook.

I had to get out of town for a while.

For a week, I soothed myself in a part of the Alps where students and young couples, whose poverty is charming and not yet pathetic, like to take holidays. My eccentricities found more spacious acceptance there. It was my custom to take my violin to a meadow and play for an audience of stones and grasses. I actually preferred the sound of the cello, but it was more reasonable for me to take up the violin, which I did when I first came to Paris as a medical student. Obviously the violin is a more portable instrument, easy to carry to a remote meadow. There was only a little time left before the first snow would cover my kind and attentive audience; the white streaks were seeping low on the lavender peaks that stood at the back of the meadow. These peaks were the clear owners of the hall. Chastised for not worshipping in my neighbors' cathedrals, I understood prayer and devotion in this and other meadows where I found solitude and impressive godlike silence and largeness. I often asked those mountains to grant me some peace. I asked them to forgive my foolish attempts to alleviate the pains and diseases of my fellow humans. I asked them to instruct me as to what improvements I could make in my techniques as a man of medicine, having a dim recollection of my intentions as a boy of becoming a skilled man of science in order to make the world and the human body clean and beautiful and painless.

The answer to my prayers came though delicate oracles, an insect on spindly legs skittering across the surface of puddle, a fox coming to the edge of the woods and yipping at my painful version of a Breval sonata.

8

Je commençais à pensar que quelque chose fermentait.

I BEGAN TO FEEL that something was simmering, that Paris was a pot of water on a flame and I was one of the live toads thrown into it. Every day when I looked out the window, the tower being built for the Universal Exposition was a little taller, its massive metal skeleton a kind of growing doom, gallows for some innocent giant unjustly condemned.

Conversations at cafés sounded nefarious to me. Prostitutes called out to me, mixing Christmas references to the baby Jesus with requests to wrap their legs around my back. The narrow streets, with basement windows and women standing half naked in doors that seemed to be sinking into the ground at a slant, were capable of entangling a man like a net. The thought of Charcot's glib and arrogant gatherings or a chaotic evening of chronic anger at the Balise dinner table made me ill, dizzy. Oscar chastised me for spending too much money eating at cafés, for the hundredth time disdaining me for not moving where we could have a kitchen and a cook. I yelled at the poor man, "For God's holy sake, man. Leave it be!"

Of course, this resulted in a sulking servant who made sure that the fire was slightly too low and the coffee set out on the table only slightly warm.

My patient the Widow gave me some solace with her intelligent enthusiasm for the upcoming exposition, which she claimed would lift all of Paris out of its gray depression, due in part to its lack of recovery from "that awful war thing" and to the violent chaos that ensued with the Commune. She claimed that the exotic colonies would indeed inject adrenaline into the slumping spirit of the society. In fact, she had redecorated her own luxurious flat in an Oriental motif that included bamboo furniture and silk pillows. When not giving me a tour of her revisions, including a standing lamp resembling a palm tree with two stuffed monkeys attached to it, she complained of stiffness in her joints but did not want to repeat the rheumatic towel treatment. I offered morphine, which seemed to satisfy her.

My own home, with the growing gallows outside the window and the sullen manservant, was unwelcoming. Hoodlums had been smashing the gas lamps at night. My bookshelf seemed an accomplice to the darkness: novelists mangled by addictions and diseases, tales of industrial horror in mines and railroad yards, Napoléonic heroes doomed to defeat. Only my violin seemed friendly to me, until I took it out of the case and found it hopelessly out of tune. This meant that I would have to take it along to some place that had a well-tuned piano, either the Widow's house or Dr. Charcot's, but I was loath to do more than the leanest of socializing required by my profession.

When I ate dinner in the cafés, one for its fish, another for its puddings, I put a copy of a newspaper in front of me, opened to keep casual intrusion at bay. At one café there would be talk all around me about the Universal Exposition, debates about its ability to show the world that the French were the leaders of art and technology, constant chatter about the aesthetic qualities of the tower, which then led to the inevitable statement that art was dead in France and had been for years. Such were the topics around the Pont Neuf cafés. At another set of cafés the arguments were about the elections to be held the next year in October and the benefits of one party over another. Always some drunk student stood up and declared the Guesdists the only purveyors of truth: he called for a revolution of workers and left forgetting his hat; or his companion, another drunk student, would rise and state that a return of the monarchy was the only rational recourse, since everything had gone to hell since Napoléon's defeat. I laughed to think of Napoléon ensconced in England, perhaps sneaking out at night to dismember some prostitute.

Sometimes I took myself to a tea shop to the west, where there might be a few farm widows and railroad clerks eating a flat egg pie and emanating a kind of peace that only acceptance of one's lot can provide. I spent Christmas at an uncle's farm near Rouen, where there was more silence than debate. Framed by a damp quiet, the same stories were repeated about my mother and father and how she had died with the third miscarriage and doted on me so, and about how my father had lived a good life afterward, having a son as a doctor whose generosity allowed him to go to his grave a plump and rested man. I always had the feeling that this story was repeated in part as an affectionate ritual, but also to remind me of the rewards of my generosity. Perhaps they were afraid that my subsidies to their finances would stop. But I always left an envelope with my year's charity to them, under the comfortable ruse that it go to the upkeep of family land.

One night in early January, after indulging in the weary quiet of one of the working-class cafés, I went to bed in my apartment with a mild nausea weakening my limbs. Oscar had gone to sleep in the hallway under the coat hooks, where he unfolded a very well-organized pile of comforters and pillows in which I sometimes had a hard time locating him. Sometime in the night, I rose to use the latrine. I felt very dizzy and had to push away images of my own brain pocked with lesions. Men of medicine have many images with which to torment themselves when they are sick, most of them learned as students examining cadavers. I shivered and quietly returned to my room, wanting privacy in which to endure whatever course my illness would take. I located the chamber pot under the bed, slippery with dust, and pulled it to where I would be able to use it simply by leaning my head over the bed. Rationally arranging the environment in which I planned to be increasingly miserable, I felt some comfort and slept, feverishly aware of my condition. I had a vivid and fantastic dream, set in a landscape totally unfamiliar to me. I remember several images from it even now: the rolling, barren hills, leading in one direction to huge mountains that looked like giant boulders and in the other direction to a river, which I could identify by the meandering line of trees. In this dream everything happened just above my head, in a low sky in which passing clouds held the characters: First two men, completely naked except for top hats, emerged, singing a hymn to me. Then horses stampeded from a cloud, hundreds of them, rumbling just above my head. They were not normal in color but red and white and black and yellow. Then the clouds were made of the faces of children crying. Icy rain was pelting my windows.

I awoke feeling mournful. And I could not tell if I mourned for my personal losses or for some universal misery. It was gray outside, so that it could have been dawn or late on a cloudy morning. I leaned with shaking arms on the windowsill and saw above the rooftops and the sticks of trees the almost completed tower. It began to glow red. It drummed like a heartbeat and sprouted red leaves. I looked down and a little fox was sitting beside me, howling like a dog. Then I knew that I was not yet awake, so I dreamed that I went to my bed and lay down again. Now I was afraid that I would never wake up. I willed myself to move, to stir enough to be aware again of my body. I woke up and saw Oscar peaking around my door.

"Oscar, am I awake?"

"It's not for me to say, doctor," he replied.

I groaned, getting up.

"I'm not well. But get me some coffee anyway, and perhaps a little bread and butter."

My nausea had formed into a pulsing headache. But by the afternoon I believed the illness to have passed. I sent word to Bicêtre that I would be a day late on my usual visit to the two men there who had been in my care before their families took the last recourse of placing them in an asylum.

I felt an increasing urge to get away from my apartment, especially when Oscar announced that he was going out for a few hours to take clothing to the laundress and perhaps have a game of cards. My clothes, as unfashionable as they are, were always immaculately clean. Nothing soiled lasted in my household for more than a few hours, for Oscar was madly in love with the laundress. He even helped her with the washing, and I know that part of the wages I gave him went to her. He described to me her household as being warm with brothers and cousins who lured him into card games and conversations about military history and strong men. His casual amusements sounded wonderful to me, and so I took off, convinced that I was cured from whatever had poisoned my system.

It was a particularly gray and cold day, when all the buildings shine dimly. Rain decided to become snow and then changed its mind again. I was sitting in a café near my apartment, risking some social interaction in order to have a good bowl of clear broth. As though on cue, a group of students burst in as soon as I had opened my newspaper. They arranged tables and grabbed chairs in order to accommodate their party. They clearly intended to dominate the place with their competing and thriving male vigor. They talked loudly, slamming the table with their hands, rocking their chairs back on two legs. Their pontifications were raucous and bound to get worse with drink. And then I saw Madou passing quickly by outside. It took a moment to understand what I'd seen, since she had never been to my apartment and I never saw her near it. For a horrifying moment, I wondered if I was still asleep and dreaming. I rose up and ran out. I grabbed her shoulders from behind. Turning around with aggressive impatience, she fell immediately into my arms and said, "Oh, Philippe! I've been looking for you! You must come. He is here. He is staying with us and he is very ill. He says he's dying."

I knew whom she meant immediately.

We took a cab to her family's apartment, and she told me that he had shown up at her door, asking to stay with her for a few days until he was well enough to find a way to get back home. He had realized, she said, that Mexican Joe had no intention of helping him to save money. He said that he knew of an Indian who'd found work on some farm in the country; to Choice's amazement, Madou told me, this misguided fellow meant to stay and live in Europe. The thought made him sick, he said. He said that

that man must not have had any grandparents. Madou reported what he said and admitted that he disoriented her and she wasn't sure what all of his words meant.

I was thinking that he was suffering some kind of neurological condition that caused delusions, speech aberrations, and ataxia. I had not yet seen the man, but I was already listing the three possibilities: epilepsy, third-stage syphilis, or neurological damage as a result of indulgence in alcohol or possibly even absinthe. There were limitless possibilities for a man's ruin in the cities of Europe. Madou demanded that I be helpful.

The Balise apartment was very silent. I thought no one was home, but in fact both mother and father were in the parlor, staring at a fire that was being poked at by their servant, Suzanne. In the corner of the room Clarisse was crocheting, sitting on a settee next to Randolphe, who was reading *La République*. The loudest noise in the room was the rattling of pages when Randolphe, with some defiance, turned them. Madame Balise stood and came toward us, addressing Madou in a fierce whisper: "We cannot have him stay here. It is just not possible, Madeleine."

The mother turned to me and said, "He has frightened Cecile to death, asking if we were going to prepare Pee-Poo for dinner."

"He was being amusing," Madou whispered back. "He wasn't being serious, Mother, for God's sake."

"Cecile is locked in her and Madou's room with poor little Pee-Poo."

Madou pulled at me. "Come on. You should see him."

She took me to the closet where I had previously seen her portraits. Now the trunks were piled in a corner and the canvases all leaned against the wall under the window. At first I saw no one there, but sitting on the edge of the cot, in black trousers, dark socks, and a white shirt, was the Indian. He stood up, his feet spread widely as though to give himself a steadier base. He grasped my hand in greeting, his own hand feeling stronger than mine. He spoke then in a combination of his own strange tongue and English, throwing in a few phrases in French. He spoke directly to me, in a consulting tone, calm and soft. But he sat back down and held on to the edges of the cot with his large hands.

Madou translated for me, "He knows that you are a man of medicine and asked to see you." A pigeon flew onto the windowsill outside, and Choice turned as though to see if it was someone he knew, only to find that it wasn't. He watched Madou speak for him and nodded, approving what she said.

"He says that he is a man of medicine as well, but as you know, it is difficult sometimes to use your skills on yourself. And besides, his powers have been drained since he crossed the water . . . came from America. He has felt his strength and his life fading more and more, and this is why he has left Monsieur Berrera. He says that sometimes his hands are very cold."

Choice held his hands out. I took them and he held on to mine, gripping them as though to express his trust in me. I was suddenly bereft of any of my previous assertions about diagnosis: his pupils were normal in size, he had no twitches, and he didn't have the distinctive odor of a man who has been consistently drunk.

I held his wrist and found his pulse, which seemed normal. I then felt under his chin for any swelling, somewhat desperate to light upon some cause for his diminishing health.

He said something and Madou translated, as though telling the most serious of his symptoms, "He cannot remember his mother's face."

Some emotion swelled in my abdomen, and I noted that the back of my throat was tightening. He continued to speak with gestures and bits of English and French, and Madou translated.

"He says that he can remember Queen Victoria's face but not his mother's, and he spends many nights without sleep trying to remember it. He sometimes feels as sick as he did when the boat left New York."

He stood up again and made a small show of wavering and stumbling on the deck of a boat. I asked Madou to leave. She hesitated, but Choice thrust his chin toward the door sternly and she left, closing the door behind her.

I then indicated to Choice to remove his shirt. He followed my instructions quickly and with dignity, not demonstrating the shame I often see in my patients, whose demeanor reverts to that of a child when they must let go of their costumes of civilization. I put my head against his naked chest to listen to his heart, which was strong and a little rapid. But then I noted that my own heart was beating at the same rate. I turned him around and listened to his back as I tapped on it for any congestion of the lungs. But I could detect nothing. There was no rash or lesion or any sign of injury that I could see. Wearing my most congenial professional smile, I held his shirt out for him to put on. I said, "You seem good, sound, healthy in the body."

He nodded and sighed, disappointed that I could not give any definition of his illness. In another case, I might tell a man something, provide him with some ritual to perform to make him feel that he is taking some control of his predicament, but this man, I was certain, would see immediately into the emptiness of such a ruse. I shrugged, and he shrugged and laughed. I nodded and left the room. Madou was just outside in the hall and asked for my diagnosis.

"I cannot say without a more sophisticated examination. I don't have my bag with me. But I would say that the problem is with the nerves."

"The nerves," she repeated, and then she rolled her eyes and knocked softly on the door. Lowering her head, she listened to his voice, and then she went in and closed the door behind her.

For a moment I stood there, hearing no voices from the room, wondering what I should do. I went back to the parlor, where heads lifted to observe me. The configuration there was little changed, except for a lack of Suzanne.

"Well?" Randolphe said, seeming amused at the whole situation, completely unconcerned.

"I can't say exactly what ails him, but he needs rest. I can say that."

Randolphe went back to scanning the paper, seeming more like an actor than a real personality, and he muttered, "He should not be staying here. He is a threat to the women of this house."

Monsieur Balise, who was in the middle of preparing a pipe, froze in his movements and stared at Randolphe. He said, "If you are suggesting that the head of this household . . ."

"These women require a great deal of supervision," Randolphe said harshly, and I could see the fear come into Clarisse's face.

Madou came in, holding herself with her arms crossed over her chest, as she was thinking with great concentration. She went over to her father and leaned against his shoulder as he continued to fiddle with the pipe.

"Since when did you take up pipe smoking?" she asked, lifting her head and studying him.

"Since now," he said, and clamped the pipe between his teeth. Clarisse rubbed her forehead as though to keep a headache at bay.

I said, "He is too ill to go anywhere. He needs to stay put for a while and rest. I don't think he's a danger."

"Who thinks he's a danger?" Madou said, standing up straight and alert. "Oh, let me guess. It must have been

Randolphe, who abhors the idea of a man with a stronger back than his strutting in his hen yard."

"Madeleine!" Madame Balise hissed.

Randolphe refused to give up the nonchalant attitude of a man reading a newspaper and said from behind it, "He's a savage, a primitive and unruly savage. The others in the building will object, and justifiably so in my opinion."

"If you stir them up," Madou said, "which I have no doubt you will do."

The mother tossed her head back and said, "Oh, I truly cannot stand the idea of his being here at all. It frightens me."

"What frightens you, Mother, what people will say?" When Madou said this, Clarisse looked up and smiled at her.

Madame Balise sighed. "I thought he was an Italian when he came to the door."

Randolphe laughed scornfully.

Madou said, "All right, then, we'll tell everyone he's Italian."

Suzanne came through the door, a log hanging from each hand. Monsieur Balise watched her carry them to the fire and said, "He can have those damned shoes, the ones . . ."

"Yes," Clarisse said. "Those beautiful Italian shoes mother bought for you."

Madame Balise smiled. "Oh, I'd forgotten those. Very expensive, dear. You have been so cruel about those shoes."

"They hurt my feet, dear, because they are . . ." He held the pipe out so as to make his point clearly. The acrid smoke went into his eyes and he blinked rapidly.

Madou and I looked at each other as the conversation became animated around the shoes, as to whether they would fit the Indian and as to whether they indeed had the Italian look to them. Suzanne's voice, like a flute suddenly appearing in a composition otherwise dominated by horns, said, "So, he is staying?"

Madame Balise said quickly, "Only for a few days."

Suzanne clenched her teeth and left the room, shutting the door hard. Randolphe was grinning as he said, "An angry servant is a home's demise!"

"I feel the urge to go to Mass tomorrow," Madame Balise called out. "Will anyone come with me?"

The answer was silence. Randolphe picked up the paper again and read out loud an article about a husband who shot his wife because he asked her to fix dinner and she refused.

9

Quelque jours plus tard, je traversais rapidement les Tuileries pour aller prendre un café avec un homme . . .

A FEW DAYS LATER, I was walking briskly through the Tuileries to have coffee with a gentleman involved in securing researchers for Dr. Pasteur's institute. For more than seven years I had nursed a longing to be a part of the sensational successes regarding cholera bacillus and anthrax bacillus, albeit regarding farm animals. In recent years, my uncle had personally benefited from the vaccination of sheep. My failure to understand the sickness of the Indian had pushed me entirely into my certainty that it was at Pasteur's institute that the most direct ways of alleviating suffering would be developed, though many in Charcot's circle disdained the detachment of research that did not involve direct contact with the patients. Humiliated by my ineptitude in the presence of a so-called primitive, I was determined to find something in my profession that would prove my civilization worthy of its dominance.

I had asked the driver of my cab to let me off at the end of the Pont Royal, since we both agreed that the day was a splendidly cloudless break in a spate of gray and misty ones. There were many people in the park, but my eye saw Madou immediately from a distance, strolling, I thought, with a middle-aged Mediterranean fellow. He appeared to be some aging ambassador that Madou was escorting, and my mind quickly reasoned out a number of possibilities, the most rational one being that the gentleman was a client at the bank where Monsieur Balise worked and that Madou had been asked to entertain him for a while. As I got close enough to see the man's face, I realized that it was the Indian, Choice, a man in his twenties, though he moved with slow and thoughtful steps. He seemed not only to have aged in demeanor but to have been reduced in size as well. Slightly inflamed skin rimmed his eyes. Madou clutched his arm, almost as though to hold him up. His smile was gentle when he greeted me with a nod, but his hand was cold and dry.

"Is he eating?" I asked, and he himself answered, shaking his head in the negative. "Old sickness," he said.

What he meant, Madou explained, was that he had been quite sick in a similar way when he was a boy. But that sickness came with dreams that informed him about his future. In fact, it was then that he had his first idea of himself as a healer. I was polite in my response to this information. But I was thinking that perhaps an inherited mental disease had surfaced.

He spread his arms out to indicate the expanse of

the city around him and said, "Here, no dreams. Just sickness."

"I thought a walk . . ." Madou began. "This is such a large park, and he is oppressed, I think, by the lack of natural surroundings."

I laughed, looking around at the sparse trees in perfect lines, led by marble men, framed by sculptured hedges and wide, barren walkways. "This is hardly an experience of natural surroundings, Madou."

The Indian pulled himself away from Madou and went to sit down on the edge of one of the statues. It was a depiction in bird-stained stone of the ancient slave Spartacus.

Madou said to me, "I am very, very concerned, Philippe."

"The man wants to go home, Madou," I said. "Perhaps we could present his case to our acquaintances and collect funds to help him."

She said, "Oh, I don't know." She looked over at him, and I saw panic creep into her face.

"Are you in love?" I asked, tenderly, but not without the old glint of humor.

Still looking at him, she said quietly, "No. I don't think so. I just feel that we, that he and I, aren't finished with one another." She looked back at me. "Do you understand?"

I didn't. But I said, "What do you like so much about him? He is from another world, Madou, quite foreign to yours and your constitution."

"That's what I like so much about him. He's from another world."

"It's not your world, Madou."

We stared at each other.

She leaned in and said, "Paris is one of the few places on earth where he can be treated by the best possible medical society. If he were to cross the ocean now, in his condition . . ."

A fight broke out between two dogs on leashes. The ladies walking them were screaming at each other, until one of them swept her pet up into her arms and walked away. Two identical men, smoking pipes and reading newspapers, sat on benches across from one another. Three boys ran past us, as an elderly couple toddled slowly up the steps toward the street. Pigeons bobbed in the walkways and under the benches.

I turned again to Madou and said, "I still maintain that rest–"

"How can one rest in my household, Philippe? Come now. And mother has taken up churchgoing again. She insists on praying with him, and he is good enough to comply. It's quite a carnival, but if one is to be sick anywhere in the world, I would think that Paris has much to offer."

Choice stood up and walked over to us.

"Listen," I said, including him as my audience, for I had the feeling that he was usually dismissed in discussions about his circumstances. "I would agree that fresh air would be a good idea. We can't go far, the season being a deterrent to any truly wild areas. But there are a few fine places just to the east. We could make a day of it and stay the night somewhere. But I don't want to be alone with him. I wouldn't know how to communicate and it would be damned awkward. I hardly know the man." I was arguing against my own generous offer, but the notion of a journey out of the city seemed increasingly reasonable given the man's mental and physical state. "Is he coughing?" I asked.

"No," Madou answered, and she bounced up and down as though to warm herself; she was a little excited. She spoke to him in their strange hybrid language, and Choice nodded, shaking my hand vigorously as though congratulating me for passing some examination question.

"Grand idea," Madou said. "Well done, Tic-Toc. Don't back out as you do."

I said, "Let's say in a couple of days. I'll check the train schedules, but it would be good to leave early in the morning. And I want at least a dinner out of this. So I'll plan on dining the night before and sleeping in your parlor."

"Good, yes. I'll make sure. Mother will be happy, really. Oh, this is grand!"

Choice strolled away, his hands stuffed into his trouser pockets. He turned around and motioned with a toss of his head for Madou to come to him. He waved at me and I waved back, thinking that he was an odd mixture of a needy case and a formidable gentleman. I could see how he might pass as an Italian. I wanted to tell him about the meeting I was about to attend, about the efforts I would be making to produce miraculous cures for all suffering.

That evening I attended Charcot's Tuesday-night gathering, bringing along my violin. A few of the attendants were dabbling in a quartet by Ravel, wanting to start a habit of playing music together after dinner. There was always difficulty in keeping to Charcot's rule of not talking about medical matters, so any additional nonmedical activity was enthusiastically promoted. However, that evening, when I presented my hat and coat at the door, I could hear Charcot himself railing against his colleague Dr. Magnan, whose use of animals in his studies on alcoholism appalled him. When I teased Charcot about breaking his own rule, Tourette took up for his mentor, saying, "This is a matter of policy and social morality. We aren't discussing the results of the experiments but the method and morality of them."

"Fine," I thought. These men were capable of justifying anything that suited them. I began the evening with a growing dislike of the whole venue. And in fact, two of the fellows who would make up half of our impromptu quartet weren't present, which was a great disappointment to me.

At dinner, after a few glasses of wine, I announced to the table that I had an interesting case, and Dr. Charcot said, "None of that, now!"

I responded that the case was about policy and morality. "In fact," I said, staring at Tourette, daring him to comment on my repeated use of that phrase, "in fact, it is about an indigenous American, an Indian, who has taken up residence in Paris after having been in some 'cowboy' carnival."

The amusing poet at that evening's dinner, a man

whose reputation was far more interesting than his poetry, which was always about the death of young women, said, "Poor man, being ripped from the bosom of his home to live in the stench of Paris."

No one paid attention to him, but his comment allowed my topic to proceed.

"This man, though he seems very intelligent, is wasting away. He claims to have been sick as a child. He becomes lethargic, doesn't eat."

Tourette pulled methodically on his beard and commented, "What about hystero-epilepsy?"

"I have thought of that," I said. "But I haven't witnessed any seizures. Well, and another interesting point is that he says that he is a physician among his people."

There was a silence as the table pondered this.

"Sounds like a delusion to me," Charcot said. "Megalomania."

"I can't say, but . . ."

Dr. Laborde, who was preparing a paper to give to the French Academy on the manifestations of absinthe addiction, leaned into the table so as to see me from the far end and said, "Philippe, you know I would look into the possibility of some history of inebriation."

"I have never seen him or heard of him as a drunk. The one time I was with him in a café, he was drinking coffee," I said.

"If he is a man of medicine himself, he must have some notion of what is wrong with him," Tourette said.

Moulon interrupted my response and said that he had

heard of primitive medicine men who claimed to suck tumors out through a person's skin. The poet commented that he would like to treat a tumor in a woman's breast, which caused everyone at the table to laugh heartily.

"There's an extensive use of herbs among the primitives," Moulon continued. In a scoffing tone he said, "They have great confidence in the magic of leaves and grasses."

"Yes, just like the use of foxglove?" I injected. "Or does the name 'digitalis' rescue the substance from being a primitive remedy?" My voice was crosser than I meant it to be, but I continued by tossing my napkin onto the table and saying, "It's amazing how we gentlemen can transform a thing simply by giving it a Latin name."

Tourette laughed and nodded.

Perhaps Moulon was manifesting his frustration concerning Madou's preferring her primitive to him. He wagged his finger at me and said, "Aah, you are falling into the romantic notion of the noble savage, when in fact they are barbarous heathens."

Dr. Laborde said, "I can't believe that at this table no one has suggested hypnosis as a treatment."

Charcot held up his hand and said, "Well . . ." And everyone laughed.

The poet stated, "Hypnosis doesn't work on the masculine mind, which doesn't have the emotional malleability of the feminine mind."

Then the discussion exploded into denouncement of the charlatans who hypnotized women in their parlors.

Charcot admitted that he had just signed a petition to allow women to enter a competition for medical students that they had been banned from. He suggested perhaps the men were afraid of their natural superiority.

"Natural superiority in what way?" the poet screeched.

Charcot responded, "Well, my dear sir, we men are able to create all kinds of poems and theories, in poor mimicry of a woman's ability to create life."

"There is no wisdom in that!" the poet scoffed.

"Oh, but I wonder," Charcot responded. "I have noticed the ability of women to observe details that my male students quite overlook. They are also able to concentrate on more than one thing at a time."

This caused the table as a whole to scoff, and Dr. Laborde told us, "Charcot has come out against ovariectomies as treatment for hysteria."

Charcot closed his eyes and shrugged, as though complacent about any resistance to his wisdom: "There is no pathological evidence for such a treatment. And the risks of surgery being what they are . . ."

"There are good theories that–" Moulon began, but Charcot interrupted, saying with slow emphasis, "Theory is good, old friend; but it doesn't prevent things from existing."

I roared with laughter. And before noting that everyone was staring at me, I called out, "Indeed!"

The table was quiet; Tourette's face was studying mine

intently, and he was nodding as though I were proving one of his own theories.

I had to repeat, "Yes, a theory is fine but it does not change the facts."

Moulon said, "I believe our Dr. Normand is becoming a savage himself."

Later in the evening, to make up to me, Moulon whispered that there was a great deal of irony in Tourette's talk about a man of medicine being able to diagnose his own disease, since there was a rumor that he was blind to his own symptoms of syphilis. Such gossip didn't endear Moulon to me any more than his rancor concerning the Indian. But I always felt I could be honest with him and so I said, "These Tuesday evenings with their cruel wit and gossip . . . they have a bitter taste to me these days."

He replied, "Yes, but if you are thinking of getting some help in securing a position at the new institute . . ." He raised his eyebrows. "Charcot may have his doubts, but he is well respected amongst the microscope boys."

When I took my leave, Charcot shook my hand and said, "You seem upset tonight, my boy. Bring your man around and I'll give him an examination."

As I trotted briskly down the stairway, I whispered to myself, "Never," and then repeated more loudly, "Never!" my voice echoing in the stairwell.

That night, while I lay in bed too cold to sleep and too tired to fetch a warming bottle, I saw as photographs flipped rapidly before my eyes a scene from my childhood.

A white goose that I favored as a sort of pet was crouching in the bushes. I discovered that it was crippled, its webbed foot bent back. I felt enormous pity for the animal. I took it home and wrapped its leg, making a kind of splint from a strip of kindling, though I can't say where such an idea came from. My toothless grandmother, who hardly ever engaged with anyone but gazed all day long out the window, was animated by my project. She helped me make a box for the goose and even brewed some herbs and had me soak rags in the tea and wrap them around the goose's leg. In a week or so, the goose began to hobble on its own and eat and swim in the little canal near my house. The depth of my satisfaction and the love for that goose for allowing itself to be healed manifested as a bliss that curiously began my sexual urges. I told my grandmother that I knew that I wanted to be a doctor, that God meant me to be a doctor.

In my bed in Paris, I sighed, remembering, even physically feeling, the certainty that there was a God and that he meant me to be something. "Sad," I whispered aloud, meaning that it was sad to have lost those certainties.

10

Quand je suis venu dîner chez les Balises la veille de notre départ à la montagne . . .

WHEN I CAME to dine with the Balise family the night before our departure to the mountains, I noticed a complicated change in the household. First, Pee-Poo raced to greet me, free from his mistress's arms, and ran around and around my legs. I said that Cecile must be ill or unconscious, to which Madame Balise responded by crossing herself and laughing at the same time.

In fact, Cecile was in the parlor, warming her hands at the fire, which Suzanne was stabbing aggressively with the poker. Cecile had just come in from walking in the Tuileries. "We are trying to take Choice out every day," she explained with tender concern. "And Madou was with her students all day." I realized that Cecile had rarely spoken in my presence except to the dog.

Another alteration in the atmosphere was the absence of Randolphe. He had not been there for several days, and Madame Balise whispered that Clarisse was very upset and that her being upset was upsetting everyone else. She was in her bed, intermittently weeping and sleeping.

"Yes," Monsieur Balise said, pointing the stem of his pipe at me. "Go in and see her. I don't want her eating poison before I can get her to Salpêtrière."

Madame Balise crossed herself again.

Monsieur Balise was in complete control of his pipe. He puffed it vigorously, tapped it firmly against the fireplace to remove the ashes, and pinched and tamped tobacco with an impressive economy of movement.

"I would think very carefully before taking her to an asylum, Monsieur Balise. I know these places–"

He interrupted me, saying, "By God, my dear doctor, go see her and you'll change your opinion. Nothing can be done for her here."

Cecile turned to me with her hands on her hips and explained: "Randolphe believes that my sister, Clarisse, that is, and Choice have been fornicating."

"Please!" Madame Balise called out.

Madou came into the room behind me and said, "Randolphe is a fool, a narrow-minded fool."

Suzanne made a noise, something between a laugh and a grunt.

"My God," Madou said. "There are courtesans all over this city having sex with any number of other women's husbands, and we are all supposed to pretend that it isn't so. The hypocrisy is astounding! If you would educate yourselves in something besides . . . besides pipes and gossip, you might understand the honest traditions of another culture. I myself would prefer open polygamy over lewd and shameful lies."

"What is she talking about?" Madame Balise asked the ceiling.

"You're our doctor. Go and see her," Monsieur Balise again insisted, this time holding the pipe stem with his teeth as he spoke.

Suzanne passed by me and said, "Dinner will be ready soon," in a threatening tone.

Clarisse's room was dark and smelled like dried roses. One candle burned at her bedside, and the heavy curtains were drawn so as to block out even the gas-lamp light from the street below. The rustling form in the middle of the bed rose up on one elbow. Clarisse said, "What are you doing here?"

"You are bedridden and I am your physician." But I stayed near the door, feeling that close examination was dangerous.

"I am not ill," she said, falling back into the nest of pillows and comforters. "I just want to die."

"Well, lying on your deathbed does not guarantee death, unless you stop eating and drinking for a very long time."

"Don't try to be funny," the pile of bedding and red hair said. "I'm in bed because I don't want to be anywhere else."

I closed the door and leaned forward a little so I could speak softly.

"Listen," I said. "You will be somewhere else tomorrow

if you don't stop behaving like this. You'll be in a place with thousands of wailing, rocking, and knuckle-biting women whose loss of dignity is paraded before a group of arrogant young men."

There was no answer.

"Clarisse, you'll come with us to the countryside. You'd best get away from your father tomorrow, and it will do you good."

"Where? It's so cold."

"A nice little place in the forest, with mountains, a little inn, and a waterfall."

"I can't, Philippe." She started crying. "If Randolphe finds that I've gone away . . ."

"That you're not suffering? Yes, I would agree that Randolphe is displeased when you're not suffering, unless it's he who is making you happy. I suppose that is some form of love, but look at the state it's got you in."

"He thinks that the Indian and I are lovers. I'm fond of him. I cannot help but take an interest in him, but I'm not like Madou. I don't have her childish imagination. Randolphe and I are suited . . ."

"Clarisse, come away with us. Let there be an intermission in this relentless drama with Randolphe. If you stay here they'll drag you to Salpêtrière."

In the silence between us, she rustled and sighed. "All right. But I don't want to have to talk to anyone."

"I understand. I'll tell them that you're coming with us."

"I'm so afraid, Philippe," she said.

"Does this man Choice threaten you? Has he shown an aggressive interest in you? I will have him hauled from here in–"

She fell back into the covers, exasperated at my ignorance. "No, no, no. I'm afraid of getting old and being alone and of seeing Randolphe with another woman. I couldn't stand it. I'd rather die."

I nodded and then told her I'd better be off to dinner and that she should eat something.

That night I experienced the mysteries of the household, the soft opening and closing of doors. I was sleeping in the parlor. At one point I heard someone in the front hall and so I wrapped a blanket around myself and investigated. It was Choice, and he was just coming in. It was well past midnight. A lamp was burning low on the hall table, and we could see each other's faces. Choice put his fingers to his lips and winked at me. I went back into the parlor and lay down on the horribly small settee, my feet hanging over the edge. My sleep was not deep but came in brief periods of dozing. I heard one door close, then another, voices, laughing. Finally a gray light seeped into the room and Suzanne tapped at the door.

"I've sent the boy to get the cab," she said through a crack she'd opened in the door.

Clarisse was already dressed and sitting on a trunk in the hallway, sipping coffee. Madou, like the huntress Diana aroused from a nap in the forest, appeared disheveled, clothed in her leather boots and a hooded cloak. She leaned against me, pretending to fall asleep, and her skin smelled like fertile, dark soil. I had a sudden notion to slip out of this journey somehow. But it was impossible to think of the two women and the Indian, no matter how Italian he appeared, navigating the changing of trains and all the luggage that was piling up in the hallway. Besides, if there was any suspicion that Choice was having it on with the sisters, I could not very well let them go off on their own. It was a ridiculous comedy of the parlor that made me cringe.

I shook my head at the baggage we were taking with us. There was the trunk on which Clarisse sat, absentmindedly patting Pee-Poo, who was sniffing around frantically. I couldn't imagine why one needed a trunk for one night away. But there were also two baskets of food, my own valise, and one carpetbag for each of the women. This outing had turned into a complicated journey. I asked Suzanne if our reservations on the steamship had been made. Not amused, she indicated that there was a small breakfast laid out for us in the dining room.

"You can't abandon us now, Tic-Toc," Madou said, hoarse with sleepiness.

Choice yawned, tapping his open mouth with his fist. I wondered if he knew what trouble he was, poor man.

11

Dans le train allant à Reims, nous étions tous silencieux.

On the train to Reims, we were all silent. There had been an unpleasant scene that each of us was privately digesting. At the last moment, Choice had asked Madou to bring her drawing box. Clarisse had burst out in anger that the whole trip was becoming a horror. Choice had laughed and infuriated her more. I helped the lanky and somewhat sooty boy, who had an unofficial position at the apartments assisting with menial chores, take the luggage to our cab. Clarisse hissed at me, as I dragged her by the elbow down the stairs behind her sister and the Indian. She told me that I was a cold, emotionless monster, and, to the extent that I had avoided all passions, I would end up a lonely and sour bachelor for the rest of my miserable life. Choice had kindly put his hand on my shoulder.

Outside in the freezing, gray morning, Madou had buried her face in Choice's shoulder and neck. Choice and I looked at each other with a resignation to the emotional chaos of women as Clarisse wept quietly and angrily and the cabdriver went about his business with a smirk.

So, for a long train ride we were mute, except for the conversations we constructed in our heads. I was seeing myself say in Reims, "Well, have a good time wherever you end up," and wandering off as the sound of Clarisse's sobbing outrage faded behind me. I tried to muster some real indignation about the interruption to my duties as a physician, but, in fact, I was grateful for the excuse to escape them.

The business of finding out the schedule for our train at the station in Reims and collecting our bags for the transfer resulted in a more comradely exchange amongst us, including some teasing about what was in the trunk. And on the new train, we settled into a compartment, congenially remarking on the emptiness of the train and how pleasant it was to travel without crowds.

"No one else is insane enough to go to the countryside in February," Madou remarked.

I was thinking of my parents and their farm and how bitterly cold the winter mornings were. The cracks on my father's hands were always filled with soot, as though someone had drawn on them with black ink. Choice and I looked at each other again, and I remembered Madou telling me that he had spent a winter of great hardship when he was a boy. His present sunken cheeks conjured the image of blizzards and starvation. I looked away, and he leaned over and took up one of the baskets of food that Suzanne had packed for us.

"Oh, grand idea!" Madou said. And we all expressed admiration and gratitude to Suzanne, admitting that in deportment she had been sullen, resentful, for some reason, of Choice's presence in the flat.

"She refuses to be alone with him, even for a moment," Madou said. "It's insulting and impudent."

Looking out the window, her chin on her fist, Clarisse muttered, "I think it's because he makes jokes about things, about Suzanne and mother getting at the cognac together in the kitchen." Turning to watch the unpacking of the meal, she finished by announcing, "Suzanne never laughs. She has not a cell of merriment."

Each of us took one of the small plates the maligned servant had wrapped in linen serviettes and one of the silver traveling cups. Taking up knives, licking fingers, rescuing a plate from falling off a lap, we availed ourselves of a roast chicken, slices of pear, bread and pâté. I poured the watered wine, and all four of us raised our cups. Choice said in French, "To your health."

After the meal, Clarisse was clearly more relaxed and conversant. She and Madou began to discuss Cecile's refusal to see a certain man who was trying to court her. Then they made jokes about their mother's new religious affectations and the altars that were appearing all over the house, on window ledges and even in the latrine. They stumbled over each other to repeat the story of the cousin who lived on the other side of the river and wore ostentatious fashions that didn't become her. A man had exposed himself to this cousin, in the Luxembourg Gardens, and she had reported the incident with studious and dispassionate detail. I smiled mildly, not daring to insert myself in any way into their conversation. Choice sat across from me, next to Madou, his arms crossed over his chest, his eyes closed. I knew or believed that he was not asleep. His back was too straight. Occasionally, when I was staring at his face, his eyes opened and he smiled and nodded. Finally, I looked past Clarisse and out the window at the passing fields and forests. Soon I was asleep. Right before I woke up, I had a dream that a dog was in the compartment with us. It was a strange breed, one side of it white and other side black. It kept trying to speak but could only whine.

When I awoke, the women were gone and Choice was still in the same position, staring at me. He seemed weary now, looking for something in my face that would help him. I leaned forward and used one of the few English phrases that I knew: "How are you?"

This made him laugh, and he took my hand and shook it with exaggerated vigor and said, in English, "Fine, fine, and how are you?"

I laughed with him. Madou and Clarisse came back into the compartment, chattering about when we should have dinner.

Clarisse asked me, "How long is the walk to the lake?" I told her it was about an hour from the little town.

She responded, now quite confident in her preferences, "I'll probably stay behind at the inn. A walk in the cold would be unpleasant to me."

"We should all do as we please," Madou announced. "Let's make this a pilgrimage. Each one of us should do exactly as we please and vow to keep whatever we do a secret."

Looking at the winter remnants of a large vineyard through the train window, Clarisse said, "There are clouds. Perhaps it will snow and we'll be stranded."

Madou continued, "I'm not talking about the kind of debauched selfish behavior that seems so desperate and dark. I'm talking about doing whatever gives us serenity. Isn't that what we all need? I am not yet strong enough to ignore the judgment of others and so I want to be somewhere where others do not judge me."

I thought about my violin. I had purposely left it behind, and now I regretted it.

Clarisse grew pensive. Choice unbuttoned the top button of his shirt.

"Then we don't have to dress for dinner or pretend to know more than we do?" I asked.

"Exactly!" Madou said, jumping a little on her seat. "You understand! We mustn't in any way ridicule, not even in a teasing way, what we choose to say or do. Of course, if what one says or does is harmful in some way to someone who is present . . ."

"This sounds suspiciously American to me," I said. "Individual liberty, only slightly curtailed by civility–a bit crude, perhaps."

"Oh, but with kindness, with the refinement of kindness," Madou pronounced.

"What do we do with our irritation with each other?" Clarisse asked.

Madou thought about it and spoke to Choice; he said a word or two to her and she nodded.

"We go off alone for a while. We dilute the irritation with solitude. It's no good spoiling everyone else's serenity."

"What if it helps my serenity to insult someone?" I asked.

Choice spoke and Madou said to me, "He says that you sound suspiciously American."

"I'm confused," Clarisse said. "What are the rules?" Madou sighed and sank back.

"Do you need some solitude, Madou?" I asked mischievously.

When we arrived at Chermoutier, the sky was hazy, but Clarisse was relieved that the clouds did not look storm laden. All of my companions seemed to have been aired out, their clothing loosened on them. Clarisse was almost joyful, chattering as I hadn't seen her chatter for years, about the charming town, its colorful timber-framed houses and Biberschwaüz tiled roofs.

"We should shop for furniture here. The colors are so wonderful," she said.

Choice seemed more substantial; he breathed deeply and looked past the houses to the foothills, carpeted with evergreen and the lacy sticks of deciduous trees. He walked to the edge of the little train platform and unbuttoned his shirt more, his cloak slung over his forearm. He looked like any man standing on a rural train platform.

I busied myself to find a fellow with a cart empty enough to accommodate that embarrassing trunk and all our bags. The little inn was not far, for nothing could be far in that small town. But it would not have enhanced my serenity to carry the trunk up the steep street, even with Choice's assistance.

A man who had just unloaded a pile of wood onto the platform agreed to take our luggage. The four of us then walked up toward our lodging. At one point, Madou ran ahead and Choice ran after her.

Clarisse muttered, "She is insane. The man has absolutely no prospects and no connections in her society."

"Perhaps that's why she is so taken with him," I suggested. And I couldn't help adding, "Wisdom is not always the instigator of love."

Clarisse tapped me on the head with her gloved hand.

She said, "I agree with Madou that we should refrain from all criticism and judgment. God knows I have had enough of it with Randolphe."

It was heartening to me to see that her eyes did not tear up when she said the Prince of Darkness's Christian name.

Madou waved at us from the entrance of the inn.

"She is such a child," Clarisse muttered.

12

Le proprietaire allemand charmait les sœurs.

THE GERMAN LANDLORD charmed the sisters. He was flushed with glee and full of admiration for our eccentric hardiness.

"No one comes for the winter," he scowled.

We were the only guests there, occupying two of the upstairs rooms, which were divided by a hall from which a stairway went directly down to the café. There was an outside latrine, which the women shrieked about. But the proprietor's sturdy wife, whose thin and wispy red hair showed her white scalp, merrily showed them the chamber pots under the bed and complimented Clarisse on her beautiful hair. She talked incessantly but amiably. All was well.

We had hot coffee and some cherry tarts with some mild cheese. I instructed my friends to change for the hike, for we had about four hours of daylight left. Clarisse said she was sure she wanted to stay behind in the warm room and read and nap.

As Choice and I were waiting in the empty dining

room, Madou trotted noisily down the stairs in layers of wool, including leggings, shortened skirt and a matching jacket, woolen gloves, and her dark, hooded cloak. She wrapped a shawl around her neck. She was a pile of wool with a face.

"I'm ready," she announced cheerfully.

We had only to keep walking up the hill behind the inn to find the trail. There were patches of snow in the shadows, the remnants of what had melted during the day and hardened into white ice at night. Choice and I plodded steadily, both of us carrying satchels. Mine held a rolled-up blanket and the remains of Suzanne's baskets. His held two empty green wine bottles filled with cold water from the pump behind the inn. After we crossed a stream, which made Madou shriek and laugh, the trail became very steep, and we all fell silent in our efforts to press on. I took up a thick branch, snapping the twigs off to fashion it into a walking stick. Choice passed both of us.

A waterfall, whose roar we could hear from a distance, invigorated Madou, who yelled above its noise, "How magnificent!"

The path became even steeper, and Madou stopped behind us, leaning against a boulder. She caught up to us when we waited for her, and then lagged farther behind.

"Oh, this is too hard," she said. "How much longer?"

Choice and I, as we often did, spoke to each other silently with our eyes. I knew what he was saying; I knew what Madou was revealing about herself to him that she was oblivious to. The vision of Madou tromping behind a band of men and women who were moving with their horses, dogs, tents, baskets, blankets, and babies through a falling snow made me shake my head. I could hear her call out, "Oh, this is too hard! How much longer?" And I could see the people leaving her farther and farther behind.

Choice turned and went to her.

"You're being a child, Madou!" I said. And realizing I had broken her rule and was judging her, I added, in my defense, "You are most definitely disturbing my and Choice's serenity."

"I need to rest," she said.

Choice dragged her by the wrist up the path. When they got to a wide stream, Madou was cursing him, stomping her foot, cursing in French, English, Indian, whatever she could lay her tongue on. He was just listening, watching her. Then he lifted her over his shoulder like a sack of raisins and walked across the large log felled over the stream as a bridge. He tossed her on the far bank. I lingered on the other side until I saw that she was laughing.

When I came to them, Madou was standing and smiling. With weary force, she followed the trail, but stopped often to catch her breath.

"I'm glad we're only doing this once," she said.

There was a steep embankment just above the lake. I watched from there as Choice walked down and stood below us on the sandy part of the shore, his hands on his hips. He was staring at the mirror-smooth water, which had a thin layer of ice on its edges, a white rim of winter. In the distance the mountain peaks were completely white.

I helped Madou manage the steep downward path, and then the three of us stood together and stared at the water.

I spread the blanket down and Madou sat on it, holding her knees and looking at the picture the lake, the pine trees, the Alpine peaks, and the boulders sprinkled along the shore made. Choice announced to us with a few words and an arcing gesture of his hand that he was going to walk around the lake. We watched him, and Madou said, "This is doing him so much good. Don't you think? I've never seen him so vigorous."

"Perhaps we should place him in a sanatorium in the mountains."

Madou stared as he disappeared where trees obscured the shoreline. "He looks like something wild, doesn't he?"

"You romanticize him, Madou."

She lay back, and I said, "Are you in love?"

She shook her head and said, "No. I won't let myself be. It's a madness. Are you?"

"No," I said.

"Good," she said. "Then we're all right."

After a while, we saw Choice coming around toward us, climbing over a giant's handful of boulders. Madou said to me, "What if I don't belong anywhere, Philippe? What happens to people who don't belong to any group or family or religion or political movement?"

I was glad that perhaps she had had an insight about herself when she couldn't keep up with her man of the Wild West. I also thought of her paintings, which represented another venue in which Madou could not excel.

"Well," I said, "I suppose one could be given a place on the outskirts of the community and status as a wizard or hermit."

"You've created your own place, Tic-Toc, your own little 'outskirts' with your profession and your books and music. I don't want to be alone like you."

"Loneliness is not the worst thing in the world, is it? What about being imprisoned with someone who doesn't admire who you are–in a society or even a marriage with people who increasingly despise you?"

Madou stood up abruptly. "Oh, stop! You are attacking my serenity with a butcher knife! Let's talk about something else, or not talk at all."

She folded her arms over her chest and waited for Choice. He appeared above me and began to take off his shirt and trousers.

"What are you doing?" I asked.

He nodded his chin toward the lake.

"He's going to go into the water," Madou said.

"I know his intentions; I just don't understand them."

Madou backed away as he peeled off the leggings he wore underneath the trousers and then stood completely naked before us. I was amazed and completely confused. His body seemed an animal perfection, while his face had the wisdom of a grandfather in it. I thought of the Egyptian god with the head of a falcon, or of the Italian clown Pantalone. It was a strange and irrational combination: a god and a clown, an Egyptian and an Italian–an association worth analysis, if one were interested in such nonsense. Choice had his hands on his hips and waited.

"Are you waiting for me?" I asked.

I could feel Madou watching. She lifted her hand slowly and rested the tip of her finger between her teeth, partially obscuring a sly smile. A bird careened from the top of a tree and across the water, dipping low and catching something in its beak.

I stood up and took off my cloak. Madou sat down on the blanket again. There was a large silence until I stood naked, almost translucently white beside Choice.

"Perhaps I am in love," Madou said, raising one eyebrow. "Or at least some parts of me are."

My skin felt lumpy and wan in comparison with the Indian's texture. He turned and ran into the water, yelling, his shriek like a predator's echoing all the way to the mountain peaks. I followed without the shriek and having to hop once when a sharp pebble got imbedded in the bottom of my foot. Madou laughed, her voice echoing over the lake.

Choice was up to his waist in the frigid water, dipping up and down. He went in completely over his head, came up beside me grinning. I was huffing, bobbing in place and laughing.

"Shrivels the genitals," he said, in French so perfect I narrowed my eyes. He then said, "Water has power."

My chattering was almost becoming convulsive.

"Move around," he said, grinning. "Swim! Move!"

"I am freezing, going numb!" I chattered. "This is insanity!"

Then he took off, swimming like a water snake. Again, I had a momentary and dizzying terror that I was dreaming. Why, suddenly, did this man speak like a French native? How had he lured me naked into a freezing lake in the middle of winter? Was he a demon? I actually considered this. I ran awkwardly splashing back to the shore. I turned, holding myself and watching Choice. My fear of him sank, and instead I had the notion that I needed him, that if I were in a dream, I needed his help to navigate it. He came out, slowly, walking, his teeth chattering in an amused grin.

Two naked men, one like the negative print of the other, walked toward our bundled little Madou, who looked us over studiously.

"Your lips are blue," she said. "In fact, I think soon you will both be of the same race of blue men."

We hunched over, picking up our clothes. Choice shook his out; I held mine to my skin, shivering, too cold to divide them and put them on.

"I love you both," Madou said. She crawled over to me. Kneeling, she bent over and kissed the tops of my feet. Then she moved to Choice and did the same, holding his ankles. She looked up at him, a child adoring him, but her arms were still circled around his ankles, and she pulled at him so that it was clear that she meant to make him fall. He stumbled back, laughing, and fell onto the cold sand. Madou climbed onto him and lay stretched out on his naked body.

I caught myself staring at them with a simpleton's smile on my face. And then Choice's eyes met mine and a transformation in mood occurred. Still looking into my eyes, Choice grabbed Madou's wrists and rolled over so that she was beneath him. He was still holding her wrists, pinning her and speaking his own language, muttering and smiling as his face got closer to her breasts, which were rising and falling quickly with her panting. Madou turned her head toward me. Her eyes were closed. She twisted her wrists in his hands, but he did not let go.

I stepped forward, still holding my clothes against me. "Here now," I began. But Choice jumped to his feet still holding her wrists, so that Madou was roughly pulled up and then turned around and pulled against him. They were both facing me, but Madou was looking down and breathing with her lips parted in an expression of concentration. Choice held her firmly against him, his forearm over her chest, the other arm across her stomach. He murmured against her cheek but looked directly and unwaveringly at me. Finally Madou looked at me as well, her eyes sleepy, and said to him, "Let me go. You're scaring Philippe." But she did not struggle against him. Choice looked behind him to where the forest began and then walked backward with her, his nose and lips against her disheveled hair as he spoke coaxingly. She held on to his forearm, stumbling a bit as she was pulled with him.

"Let her go," I said. "It's time to go back."

Choice stopped but did not free Madou.

A sudden stillness descended upon everything. The lake, the wind, the birds went silent; I felt as though the trees were waiting, watching and daring us in the context of a vast isolation. The three of us knew that any number of things could be said or done at that moment and never known to the outside world. I kept my clothes tight against my body, for I did not want to reveal that I was aroused.

Madou reached her hand out to me and said my name. It was a plea, but I cannot say for what. Choice lowered his hand from her stomach and pressed against her pelvis, pushing her hips against his. Madou closed her eyes again.

"We should go." I turned away from them. I heard Madou's voice, but I was humming a portion of a Bach cello sonata and could not tell what she said.

And then Choice walked past me and stood looking out over the lake.

When I was dressed and turned toward Madou, she was brushing at herself. She seemed to be avoiding any exchange of words or glances with me. Choice grabbed his clothing with aggressive disdain and dressed facing the water.

As we collected the blanket and satchels, Choice took up a pebble and squeezed it hard in his hands. Wind rattled the trees. As though a spell were broken, Madou sighed and rested her head against his back. I pointed out that the sun was deep in the sky behind us. Choice walked with forceful strides ahead of us, then ran up the steep incline to the path. As we headed back on the trail, my skin tingled as though electrified. I did feel invigorated; I did feel very alive.

13

Clarisse était assise dehors sur un banc qui était adossé au mur blanc de notre auberge.

CLARISSE WAS SITTING outside on a bench against the white wall of our inn. She had changed for dinner into a dark green dress whose hem we could see beneath a layer of cloak and shawl. In both gloved hands she held a cup of chocolate, which warmed her face with steam. She laughed at us.

"You look exhausted," she said, "like children who have been lost in the forest."

Madou sat next to her and put her arm around her sister's shoulders. "Oh, I could live here," she said. "It's so quiet."

Clarisse admitted that she had had enough of her own company. "I was glad to see you come around that corner," she said.

Choice went upstairs, and I said to the two sisters, "I think Choice is more able in our language than he lets on."

"People use words for a lot of nonsense," Madou said. She stood up and went inside as well.

When I went up to my room, I did not see Choice and immediately assumed that he and Madou were alone together in the other bedroom. I hummed to myself a soprano's passage from Mozart's *Magic Flute*. In fact, I put on a little show for myself, at one point singing softly in falsetto. And so I was chagrined when I went to the window to close it and saw that all along the Indian had been a few feet away, sitting out on the roof of a shed right beneath our window. I myself had sat in that same spot several times when I was staying at that inn and unable to sleep. Alone, I had watched the constellations creep across the sky and wondered about the passage of time.

I leaned out and said, "It's time to eat, my friend." I pantomimed lifting a fork to my mouth. He nodded.

At the dinner table we drank to our adventure and our friendship. Choice laughed at the cloth flowers on the mantle and at the clock, which was stuck at half past nine. The landlord and his wife served us and a soldier who ate by himself at another table. The young man in uniform was serious and came and went without engaging us. He was no doubt full enough of conversation. The proprietress had stood by his table as he ate, commenting on Napoléon, the grape harvest, her brother's child-raising errors, and a number of other topics. At our table, we exchanged looks of amusement and pity for the suffering soldier. "He probably wishes he were in some battle," Clarisse whispered before her bent wrist with bread in her hand.

At one point the sisters and I discussed Choice, in his

presence, but with a presumption of his inability to contribute to the topic, even though he was the topic.

"He upsets Suzanne," Madou announced, cutting the broad noodles beneath a heap of stewed beef and carrots. "She is offended by his inclusion at the table. I can tell."

Clarisse said, "Ha! I told you, she is offended by the fact that he caught her and my mother at one of their little drinking parties in the kitchen. Suzanne thinks he means to do some horrific crime in our house. She doesn't believe he's ill."

"Your mother seems to have traded her brandy parties for religion. Perhaps that is an improvement," I said, for I wanted the conversation to take on a more philosophical and less personal tone. But I have noted that it is difficult to drag women away from the trough of personal confession and opinion.

"What is wrong with him anyway, Madou? How long is he going to live with us? It's very strange. He's not a relative, after all." Clarisse bent over so that the noodles slipping from her fork would fall back onto the plate and not onto her lap.

Madou had finished her stew and was tearing off a piece of bread. "You'll excuse me, I hope, if I tell the truth."

"But we are all free here," I said. "Do so with impunity, Madou."

Her mouth full of the bread, she said, "What is wrong with Choice is the same thing that is wrong with you, Clarisse. His nerves are under duress. He is afraid, but being a man, he is as much disturbed by the fact of his fear as by what causes the fear."

I said, "Well, so you are saying that men have a double fear–the initial one and then the fear of the fear itself."

"Oh, yes," Madou responded.

"I think there is a deterioration of some organ or tissue at work," Clarisse said. She pushed her plate away. "I think it is highly unkind not to avail the man of the medical expertise in our society. What do we know of his family, of some malady he's inherited?"

Madou began to speak, but Choice stopped her in a surprising way. He covered her mouth with his hand. It was a gesture that had a criminal appearance, as though he might be in the process of dragging Madou upstairs and doing some violence to her. I felt an annoying thrill as the two of them looked at each other, Madou's eyes steady and without panic above his large hand. When he took his hand away, Madou's smile was revealed. She stood up and said, "I'm going for a walk in the village."

Clarisse carefully smoothed her napkin down on the table and said, "Grand idea. Let's walk and then have dessert and some German liqueur, something unpatriotic."

When we were leaving the inn, the proprietress walked briskly toward Madou with a smile on her face, and Madou pretended to have a coughing fit and not see her. She slipped outside with us, and we all laughed at the blatant maneuver to escape the woman's entrapping monologues.

A few of the town's windows and a thin moon gave off some light as we meandered up the one street, behind us a church and in front of us a cow pasture. Choice walked ahead, his hands clasped behind his back. Thunder rumbled to the east, and I stopped to assess the location of the clouds that so far had not obscured the moon. Clarisse and Madou leaned into each other, muttering plans for our departure the next day. I watched Choice's dark form, the hair blown a little. I pressed my hat down farther on my head and wondered whether there was any reason a top hat was less foolish than a nest of feathers sitting on one's head. Catching up to Choice, I put my hand on his shoulder, and he put his arm around my neck and pulled me roughly close to him, like a fellow student. We walked like this for a moment and both felt a wind come up. A light flickered inside a bank of clouds, and then thunder roiled in it.

"A man must have something to occupy him," I said, separating from him.

He gave me a look of pity. Then he shrugged.

"When we return to Paris," I said, making each word clear, "you can come with me . . . with me. You can help me with my patients . . . help me with sick people."

He stopped and grabbed me by the shoulders. A great crack of thunder stunned both of us. I could feel his hands gripping my shoulders more tightly. Then he fell to the ground.

Madou ran up, Clarisse walking swiftly behind her.

"What happened?" Madou kneeled beside him and

called to him in his own language, trying to raise his head up.

I knelt beside her and called to him. I could see his eyelids fluttering.

"Help me to take him back," I instructed, and Madou and I got on either side of him and helped him get to his feet. He was groaning, semiconscious.

The German fussed to get the door open and clear our way to the stairway. "Shall I get the doctor?" he said.

"I am a doctor," I told him.

He ran upstairs and lit the lamps in our suite.

When we got Choice into the bed, Clarisse and Madou and I debated how to proceed.

"I think he's had an epileptic seizure," Clarisse said.

"You could be right," I admitted. "Rest is important now. He needs rest."

"Yes," Clarisse said. "We all need rest. I'm exhausted."

Madou told Clarisse to go to bed, that she and I would stay up for a while. And when we were alone, sitting in chairs near the window, she started crying.

"He'll be all right, Madou," I said.

She said, "No, no, he won't be all right. He won't be all right until he goes home. I know that. I know that. And I can't . . ."

"He has gotten some sickness and needs medical care."

"What medical care can be given here?" she hissed.

"I mean in Paris. You yourself said . . ."

"I mean in Paris, too. I don't see any help for him in

Paris. All I see is him getting a very fine autopsy. I see him dead in some morgue, where some doctors smoking cigars discuss his organs." She used her sleeve to absorb the tears that came out of her eyes.

I was surprised at her change of opinion on the benefits of Parisian medicine and extended the point by saying, "Then perhaps he must get back to his own home. He doesn't belong here, Madou."

"And what will I do?" She leaned forward, her eyes wide and demanding. "What will I do when he is gone?"

She settled back and said, "Besides I don't have the money . . ."

"Please, Madou," I said. "It's not a matter of money and you know it."

She started weeping harder. "I can't," she said.

"What can't you do? You are beginning to sound like Clarisse. Tell me, Madou, are you in love with this man? Have you had relations with him?" I hated my tone, which felt perverse, almost wicked in my mouth.

"Don't become the inquisitor with me, Philippe. Don't you do that." She sat up straight, sniffing hard. "I am not a criminal. I am trying to help him. I would be terribly lonely if he were to go."

"And so what are you thinking of doing, Madou? Are you going to marry him and get him a job in the bank?"

She fell back into the chair and looked away from me.

"I am going to go with him. I am going to save money and the two of us will go back to his people together."

I let the idea float around the room. She repeated it, looking at me.

"Will you marry him?" I asked.

She looked away again and said, "I don' know. I just know that I don't belong in Paris."

"Do you belong in a settlement of Indians?"

She hated me; hatred was gathering in her eyes, and she let me see it.

"I might," she said.

"Madou." I got on my knees, my hands in her lap, as though she were an altar. "Madou, listen to me. Perhaps you are trying too hard to belong to some human thing. Perhaps it is ideas that you belong to, and activities and adventures."

"But I don't want to be alone," she said.

"You and your sister . . ."

"I don't want to end up with a man like Randolphe, or some other Frenchman who wears a top hat to make himself larger than he is and who has traded firm flesh for firm ideas."

I rocked back into my chair and sighed.

"Well, I'm insulted."

She glared at me.

"What do you belong to, Philippe? You seem more and more disdainful of your colleagues and your patients."

"Do you really want to know?"

She nodded.

"I have been thinking, you see, of just that." I looked

at Choice's very still form on the bed. "I want to know that I have somehow alleviated suffering, not in the way of placing a bucket beneath a leaky roof, but actually repairing the roof."

Her face showed confusion.

"I envy him."

"Him?" Madou looked with me at Choice. I felt that he was engaged with us in the conversation though he was still, his face in a dim wash of lamplight.

"Yes, because he is certain of what his purpose is. Even though it is by virtue of being taken away from it, he has a passionate conviction about what he should be doing. I wish that I had that. I remember when I was a child . . . when I first realized that I wanted to be a doctor . . ."

"What has changed?"

"Well, I have gotten lost in a variety of assumptions that really aren't mine but are someone else's, so convincingly presented as to make me believe that they are mine."

"What kind of assumptions?"

"For example, the assumption that any cure must be extreme and cause as much suffering as the disease, or more. Yes, that is an underlying assumption that I have noticed in my colleagues. Force and a kind of coldness in our methods are considered fundamental aspects of our profession. And I have adopted these assumptions and indeed acted upon them until, quite honestly, I find my own profession distasteful."

Madou had calmed down, distracted by my dilemma, and so I continued.

"I believe in science. I believe in knowledge and the application of that knowledge to cure disease and dysfunction. But I think that it is arrogance and not knowledge that we more often apply to our patients. In fact, I have seen with my own eyes renowned physicians dismiss the facts, as demonstrated clearly by the patient before them. And I have seen them completely dismiss the patient's own revelations of his symptoms as though a grown man were too ignorant to know where the pain in his own body lay."

Madou sighed. "Perhaps I've done something similar with Choice."

"Perhaps so," I said.

"And what is worse," I had to add, for now my mind was frantic with conclusions, "is that the patients themselves learn to doubt their own sensations. They surrender their reason to the authority of the doctor. Then all doctors are expected to sweep into their bedrooms, dispense some mysteriously effective concoction, and provide some Latinate diagnosis when often the problem will be resolved most efficiently by sensible care and time."

My pontification wearied Madou. She stood up and said, "I'm going to try to sleep. Will you call me if . . ."

"He'll be all right," I said, wide awake and embarrassed by my energy, surprised by the clarity of convictions I didn't even know I had.

"He is such a long way from his family." Madou looked down at Choice's face and stroked his head.

"Just let him sleep," I told her.

And so we did. I lay next to him for a while. I had a fitful night and only knew I slept at all because I had a dream about a man with blue skin sitting out on the shed roof. I awoke alone in the bed. At some point during the night, Choice had made himself a nest on the floor. It was early dawn, and the quiet of the place was immense and deep. I got up quietly, wrapping myself in a thin comforter. I opened the window and crawled out onto the roof of the shed. There I sat, my breath fogging the air, watching the various shapes and colors of the place transformed by the subtle increase of light.

14

Le train était deux heures de retard.

THE TRAIN WAS two hours late. A porter with a very pointed waxed mustache was breathlessly apologetic. Perhaps he interpreted our group's silence as a sullen and dangerous disapproval of the breach of schedule. But, in fact, the four of us had awoken and eaten our breakfast with that same silence. Clarisse spoke for three of us when after drinking half of her coffee she said, "I feel that I've been here for a year and that I shall miss it, though I know that as long as Paris exists I must be part of it." Choice was ravenous, politely asking each of us if we were finished with the bread and jam before consuming it all with a thick layer of butter. Then we each used the few hours before boarding the train for solitary activities. Clarisse bought a pastry at the baker's shop and then went to a furniture maker's shop. Madou sat outside on the bench and drew sketches of the street and the surrounding landscape. I went to the path and saw Choice walking ahead of me, putting more and more distance between us, though he seemed to be walking slowly. I had the notion that he was getting away from us and that he wouldn't show up at the station. I wondered if I should keep an eye on him, to make sure he came back. In fact, he somehow managed to return to the inn before I did, though I did not pass him on the path. And I had sat for a while by the waterfall.

"Perhaps we could stay another night," was the only thing that Madou said to me before we went to the little platform to catch our train.

"I have to get back, and it would worry your mother if we didn't return," I said.

Nothing was said about Choice's collapse. But Madou clung to him. On the train I drifted in and out of sleep. Clarisse stared out the window. Madou and Choice entwined themselves as much as was decent.

Sometimes I was not asleep but kept my eyes shut and thought about a number of things: my violin; my patients; my employee, Oscar; my need for a new jacket. After the change of trains in Reims, Madou sat across from Choice and sketched his face as he looked out the window. Clarisse slept next to him, her head supported by the window and Choice's cloak.

Randolphe was waiting at the outside door of the apartment house when we came to the Balise residence at dusk. Clarisse's lips trembled. As though there had been no separation, Randolphe, with a proprietary air, took Clarisse's bag and called out to the cabdriver to unlash the trunk, as though the man needed such instruction. Madou mumbled to Choice, who pressed his eyes with his fingers and nodded. I asked Madou to give my regards to her mother and father, feeling that the entanglement in the lives of this family had become uncomfortable. I wanted to assure myself that my life's routine was still intact.

Then Cecile came around the corner, Pee-Poo leading her on the leash. Seeing me, she raised her hand and called out, "I've just been to an incredibly interesting meeting of the Society for the Protection of Animals. Your friend Dr. Magnan, it seems, is abusing dogs with absinthe." I noted that when the usually quiet Cecile did speak, she was not very skilled at the subtleties.

I confessed to no knowledge of his studies and to an overwhelming exhaustion with an oncoming headache. I bid her good evening. I told the cabdriver, as we crossed the Seine, that sometimes social obligations became oppressive. He agreed with me, for I believe that it is a cabdriver's duty to agree with whatever opinion his paying customer is promoting. But before I left the cab, he confessed that his little son had recently died. I said nothing, and he drove his empty cab to the stables.

I dined that evening at a little café near my flat that was advertising an inexpensive roast lamb with mint jelly. I could not pass it up.

15

Je me suis immersé dans deux choses: ma profession et ma musique.

I STEEPED MYSELF in two things: my profession and my music. Indeed, constantly sitting on the hallway table ready to be picked up on my way out were my doctor's bag and my violin case. I dreaded the messenger boy and the notes handed to me by Oscar. I retreated into my bedroom when someone knocked on my door. I did not want any summons from the Balise family in particular. There were others I avoided as well, on the street. For example, when I saw the prostitute who had enlisted my help for the amputation case, I bowed my head and trotted briskly across the street so as to appear too preoccupied to notice her. I did not want to hear the bleak news of that man and his household.

I attended an interesting lecture on the detection of tumors, where I made a direct connection with a fellow who was administering the staff at the new Pasteur Institute. I made it clear that I was interested in work, especially concerning vaccinations.

Something was fermenting inside me. I even had physical manifestations of that fermentation in the gaseous state of my digestive system, which gave me a great deal of discomfort. Oscar suggested that I stop eating onion soup, advice which, in fact, did help a little.

I was on my way one morning to attend to the Widow and the syphilitic writer, since they lived in the same arrondissement. Oscar was buttoning my collar in the hallway when someone whose footsteps we had not heard knocked on the door. I looked at Oscar in terror, and he looked at me with weary annoyance. With a questioning expression, he indicated the direction of the bedroom. I shook my head in the negative and nodded at the front door as I retreated into the front room and took a last swallow of the cold coffee.

I heard only Oscar's voice, and then he was standing near me saying, "There is some old Italian gentleman here to see you."

My eyebrows lowered in confusion, and Oscar shrugged. He then escorted the gentleman a few steps into the room. It was Choice. Indeed, the limp and loose fit of his trousers and jacket and his stooped posture made him seem like a old man, but his face was the smooth and bony geometry of the young man I hadn't seen for a few weeks. He grabbed my shoulders and pressed one cheek against mine and then the other.

"Good morning," he said.

"Good morning," I answered. And then we stared at each other. He moved toward the window and stood looking out, his hands in his pockets. I joined him.

"They finally finished the tower. The tower is finished," I said.

"A dead tree," Choice remarked.

"Yes. I see what you mean. Yes. I understand."

"Sick people today?" he asked.

"Yes."

"I will come with you, as you said."

"Aah, yes. I remember. Yes. I agree. Of course. Come with me. Yes–two patients today in fact."

My routine suddenly seemed infused with entertaining possibilities. I quickly ran through the approach in my mind. It would be all right to tell the syphilitic writer that I had brought an indigenous American man with me, but I had better maintain that he was Italian to the Widow. Though she had a love of the exotic, she preferred it dead and stuffed, like the taxidermist's monkeys on the lamp she had in her parlor.

Choice stepped backward and placed his hand on his chest.

"Yes. Perhaps you can help," I said congenially, and immediately heard the patronizing tone in my own words. This man must have been weary of people speaking to him as though he were a child.

"All right then. We shall go!" I was cheery and excited.

I slapped one of my extra top hats onto Choice's head as Oscar came in with a bucket of water. We hurried out.

As we walked toward a cab, I said to Choice, "You know the city well it seems." He didn't respond but put his hand on the flanks of the cabdriver's horse, a large brown animal whose tail was swatting at flies.

"Don't touch the horse," the cabdriver said between coughing fits. I scowled at him, wanting to say something like, "This man knows more about horses than any cabdriver in this city," but there was no other cab in sight, and so I simply climbed in and told him where we were headed. As we passed the military grounds where I had first seen Choice, I looked down and saw that instead of bringing the medical bag, I had grabbed the violin case.

"Christ Almighty," I muttered. Choice's eyes widened quizzically. I held up the violin. "I made a mistake." He nodded and smiled. "Damn it all, and I'm late. Well, I'll have to make do, and besides, it's an excuse for not having any nonsense about ether with that madman."

I wasn't sure how much of what I said Choice understood, but our conversation was interrupted by a breeze that brought on it the distinct smell of sewage.

"Human shit," Choice said.

"Yes." I said.

When we got to the Widow's house, she was too weak to receive us in her parlor. She lay in extreme exhaustion, according to her robust maid, who showed no concern about my companion and in fact included him in her description of her mistress's symptoms. We passed through the parlor, which had become a jungle of bamboo furniture, silk wall hangings, and tropical plants in various stages of choking to death. I tapped Choice on the shoulder and pointed at the infamous lamp shaped like a palm tree, with the two stuffed monkeys climbing up it. Their eyes had the eerie shine of hypnotized demons. I shivered theatrically to indicate my response to the object, and Choice lay his hand on the back of one of the monkeys. I didn't tell him that the old woman had actually named the two mummified creatures: Boris and Jimmy.

The Widow sat up, the loose, crepe paper skin under her arm exposed for a moment as she pulled her bed jacket up. She smiled and said, "I am so glad you came. Did Marie tell you that my legs have been aching?" I took her hand gently and said, "You're looking well."

"No, I'm not. Don't you think I have mirrors, dear Dr. Normand? I am an old woman, and thank God I am rich. But that hasn't done a thing for my misery. My legs are in almost constant pain. Do you have some medicine that would help?"

Choice was lingering behind, his hands held behind his back.

"Who is that man?" the old woman said, peaking around me.

"Buongiorno," Choice said, removing his hat and holding it against his thigh.

I kept looking at him, pressing my lips together so as not to laugh. When I looked back at the Widow, she asked again, "Do you have some medicine?"

I laughed, too loudly, and said, "You know, the oddest thing! I left the house and picked this up instead of my bag!" I lifted the violin case. She stared at it. And then she looked at Choice.

"Does he play an instrument?"

I looked at Choice.

"No. No. I don't believe he does."

"Well, then," the woman sighed. "Why don't you play something for me, dear. That would be nice."

"Play something?"

"Yes," she said, wincing and leaning forward to rub her legs. "On the violin."

"Oh, well . . ."

Choice came to us and took the violin case from my hand. Sitting on the bed, he opened the case, drew out the violin and the bow, and handed them to me. He then began to rub the woman's lower legs and nodded for me to play.

I stood still, the instrument hanging from my hand as their two faces looked at me. Choice nodded again, and the old woman leaned back, saying, "Oh, that feels very good."

I shook my head, breathed heavily, and played one of the first tunes I had learned as a student, which I was least likely to butcher: a little tune by Mozart, which he probably penned when he was three. I played it three times, until I saw the woman's feet keeping time beneath the covers.

"Do you know any Strauss?" she asked.

"Well, Strauss sounds very feeble on one violin . . ."

"Play it anyway. Go ahead."

Choice nodded, still rubbing her legs.

When I had played a little bit of a waltz that may or may not have been by Strauss, the old woman clasped her hands over her chest and said, "Oh, I love that melody!"

She pulled herself out of the covers and sat on the edge of the bed. Choice stood up and helped her to stand.

"Play it again, will you, my dear?"

I played it again, and the old woman stood swaying, her eyes closed.

The maid came in and watched, skeptical and concerned.

The Widow laughed and fell back to the edge of the bed.

"Why don't we have some tea and cakes in the parlor?" she asked, and the maid began to move to the door. I held up my hand and said, "No, no, it's getting late. I'm already late to see another patient." In fact, I was eager to try this cure on the writer, excited that I had perhaps found some elixir, some combination of things that would exceed the success of the hypnotists.

The Widow walked us out and asked Choice if he had seen the marvelous monkey lamp. "I am going to leave it to Dr. Normand. I think it has some scientific value," she said.

I thanked her and had the eerie feeling that Boris and Jimmy turned their heads to watch us as we left.

We strolled down the boulevard laughing softly; I said a few words, lifted the violin, shrugged. Choice smiled.

The frantic little woman who attended the writer immediately said, before even letting us through the door, "Who is this man?"

"Mademoiselle," I said, pushing past her, "he is a healing man from one of the tribes in America. I think your employer would be greatly interested in meeting him."

"He is very distraught today. His younger brother has died."

I stopped walking and faced her, both of us understanding the implications of what she had told me. For the man's brother's death was simply a preview of his own doom, since they had the same disease.

"Well," I said. And then Choice and I were led into the man's bedroom.

There was a strong odor in his room of apple vinegar and burning metal. It was dark, as usual. The writer was wearing a patch over one eye, and he complained that he could not move one of his legs. I sat down on the edge of the bed and began to rub that leg. He pulled himself away from me and screamed, "What in hell are you doing? You physicians and your torture! What are you doing?" I stood up. Choice was standing as he had in the Widow's room at first, near the door, his hands clasped behind his back.

"And what is that? What have you put on the bed? It looks like a violin case."

"It's the damnedest thing," I said. "Instead of my bag . . ."

"Are you telling me you have no medicine?"

I tried to speak, understanding that perhaps I should suggest that I would return later that day with my bag, but he grabbed the violin case and was about to throw it. Choice came to take the thing from him and then stepped back with it and stood by the door again like a manservant. I held out my hands to him in frustrated supplication. Choice shrugged.

"And who is this wild man you've brought into my house?" the writer bellowed.

Again I could not speak before he interrupted, this time to sit up as straight as he could and point to the door: "Get out! Get out! Don't come back!"

Choice opened the door for me and then followed me out.

The fierce little woman appeared, her eyes shining like the monkeys'.

"What have you done to him?" she inquired.

"I'll send some morphine around later," I said.

Choice and I left.

Outside I breathed deeply. He held out his hand.

"Payment?" he asked.

I had to wait a moment before fully understanding what he meant. And then I was shocked.

"You want payment? For what? For today? You think I should pay you for coming with me today?"

He nodded.

Looking into his eyes, I said, "You want to go home. It's all you want at this point, isn't it." I fished in my pockets and extracted a five-franc note, which I slapped onto his palm. He put it in his trousers and then removed the top hat and handed it to me.

A woman passed by with a small dog on a leash. She'd tied a white lace bow around its neck, which drooped down as the creature sniffed at a spindly tree. Choice lit a cigarette and went to the woman. He grabbed her upper arm, and the dog began to bark in hoarse and frantic squeaks. The woman tried to pull away, but Choice's grip was firm. In a panic I shook my head and yelled for him to come to me. The cigarette was in his mouth, his eyes narrowed against the smoke. The little dog was now defecating with shaking loins, and Choice pointed to it and then put the same hand over his own chest. "Me," he said, pounding himself and letting go of the woman. She ran off, the little dog dragged on its side by the leash until she stopped and picked it up. "Me," Choice repeated.

I went home alone in the cab, with two top hats and a violin case. Oscar prepared my evening attire as though I were going to Charcot's house for the regular Tuesday-night gathering. "I'm not going," I told him.

Choice did not repeat his visit.

16

J'ai rencontré Madou et sa mère pendant un enterrement au Père-Lachaise.

I ENCOUNTERED MADOU and her mother at a funeral I attended in Père-Lachaise. A young man whose family I attended had died of a gunshot wound while "cleaning his gun." This was the euphemism so often used to refute the obvious suicide. It did not seem to confound anyone that he had been cleaning his gun while in the bathtub. Madame Balise was working her rosary the way her husband worked his pipe. Madou was weeping quietly and holding on to her mother. Afterward the three of us had some tea and brandy in a nearby café. We sat outside keeping our cloaks on. When I asked about Choice, Madame Balise said that she prayed for him constantly, that she did not think he would live another winter in Paris.

"He really must be sent home," I said. "He is not a pet, Madou."

Her nose and neck reddened and she stood up. "I think it is not your business, Philippe, since you hardly attend to my family any longer."

My heart rate increased markedly. Madame Balise put her hand on my arm and said, "She's upset. Please don't worry, Philippe. Madou, please."

But Madou was a cat pulled from the canal now. "How dare you?" she said. And she walked away.

I went after her, telling Madame Balise that I would return. Madou was marching toward the Place Gambetta. I had to run to catch up to her. I spoke to her, but she would not answer.

We walked beside a café, those who saw us no doubt believing we were lovers quarreling. Inspired, I grabbed Madou from behind, turned her and kissed her mouth. Jerking away from me, she was surprised enough to be still, and I said, "Are you in love?"

"No, no, no, no," she yelled, and even in Paris I was afraid that we were making too much of a drama in public. I shook her a little and said, "Calm yourself."

"You calm yourself. You are so fiercely dispassionate that you are a monster."

"Come on," I said, still holding her shoulders firmly. I turned her around and walked her in the direction of the café, where her mother was waiting for us. As we were about to cross the street, I said, "I want to show you something."

I pointed at a sign in a shop window. She glanced at it and then looked away. I pulled her over. It was a butcher's window, and standing amongst a display of sausages and hanging ribs was a large poster. She struggled to move, and I stood behind her, forcing her to stand still and look at what was in the window: a depiction of a bison on the run, two sharp horns curving up from the sides of its burly head. In the background were others of the herd in an apparent stampede. Inset in an oval in the middle of the big bison's large humped body was a portrait of the head of a venerable-looking cowboy with a neat goatee and mustache. His long white hair flowed from beneath a cowboy's hat. Only three words were on the poster in large white and red letters: I am coming.

Madou forced her way out of my grasp and ran across the street.

17

Un mot de Clarisse arriva pendant que je prenais mon café.

A NOTE CAME FROM CLARISSE as I was drinking my coffee. I heard the breathless voice of the boy who did errands at the apartment house where the Balises lived. Oscar handed the damp paper to me, saying, "Apparently it's urgent and you are needed right away."

I stood up and read the note, which told me that the Indian had collapsed that morning and had not regained consciousness as of twenty-five minutes ago. The boy, his blue eyes very pale in his dirty face, was waiting for me. Carefully aware that I was taking my bag, and not the violin, from the hall table, I went with him to the street, where we hired a cab.

When I arrived at the Balises' apartment, Pee-Poo was barking hysterically. Madame Balise was rocking back and forth on the settee in the parlor. Cecile was chastising Suzanne for something in whispers. Choice was lying on the dining room floor, Madou sitting on a footstool beside him. She looked up at me and then stood and stepped back from him.

"Tell me what happened," I said, getting out my stethoscope.

"What are you going to do with that?" she asked.

"Listen to his heart," I said. "Tell me what happened."

"We were sitting down to breakfast. He was holding my hand underneath the table, gripping it as though to keep from drowning. He said that he felt well, strong, though he'd mostly been lying on his cot for the last few days. Clarisse was standing behind him, combing his hair. He had gotten dressed up and said he wanted to go out today. And then he looked up at the ceiling and said, 'Madou, the roof is moving.' Then he fell to the floor."

Randolphe stepped into the room; Clarisse was behind him.

"Randolphe, help me to carry him to his bed," I said.

"No. Take him to my room. Let him stay in my bed," Clarisse said.

And so Randolphe, solemn as an altar boy, helped me to lift the man and carry him to the bedroom next to the parlor, where he continued his very still sleep.

Madou said, "Oh, dear God, he's not breathing."

"He's breathing, Madou. His heart is beating. Remember in Chermoutier; the same thing happened, and all he needed was sleep," I told her.

"But this is different. His skin is losing its warmth as though he's dead," Madou said.

Clarisse held her sister. Cecile watched, holding

Pee-Poo. Madou told the story of what had happened again.

When I lifted his eyelids, his eyes were rolled back in his head. I tried to arouse him with smelling salts, but he made no move, not even to turn away from their vapors.

"He seemed so happy today," Madou said.

"We should just let him rest, Madou." Clarisse said.

Madou touched his mouth with her fingers. I exchanged a look with Clarisse

"What shall we do if he dies?" Madou said, "What shall we do?"

I didn't know if she were asking about the logistical issues or the emotional ones, and so I simply said, "Clarisse is right. We must just let him rest. I'll be back this afternoon with another doctor. Has he . . . when he goes out at night . . . have you noticed any signs of intoxication?"

Madou shook her head vigorously. "He has been here. He has hardly been out of his room."

"Are you sure?" I asked. "Not even at night when everyone is asleep? Because when I was here–"

Cecile said, "Madou would know."

Madou said, "He has not been out for days."

"You must make sure that he takes water regularly. If he cannot drink it, soak a cloth in water and press it to his lips. Do you understand?"

Both women nodded.

I returned in a few hours by myself, hoping that he would have improved as he did in Chermoutier. But there was no change in him.

"I thought you were going to bring another doctor," Madou said.

"I will. I was hoping . . ."

His heartbeat was weaker, almost imperceptible. Madame Balise asked me to dine with them and so I did, in silence with the others as Suzanne, moving like a terrified ghost, crept around with the serving dishes.

"I said from the very beginning . . . ," Monsieur Balise said before putting a piece of chicken in his mouth and chewing aggressively.

"I have some affection for the poor man," Madame Balise said. "He is Christian, you know."

Madou said, "Mother, I told you that that buffalo man made everyone become Christians. They had to sign papers before he'd hire them."

"But he has gone to Notre Dame with me; he asked the priest there if he had been to the land where Jesus died. He seems most devout to me, a devout man."

Madou, who could not eat, slumped back into her chair and said, "It makes no difference."

Madame Balise protested, "But of course it makes a difference. It makes a very big difference. I think we should get one of the priests from la Madeleine. If the man is dying . . ."

Madou got up from the table and left. Cecile, without Pee-Poo on her lap, stared at me and then asked, "Is he dying?"

I shook my head. "It doesn't look hopeful to me, I'm afraid."

Clarisse sighed loudly and said, "What have we done?"

"What do you mean, 'What have we done?'" Randolphe said. Then he laughed. "We have allowed him to stay here without any payment, taking what he needs and asking nothing from him. We have given the man charity."

Clarisse looked at her man studiously, and then she tapped her lips with her finger as though she were figuring something out.

"You have never liked him. You make fun of him. I think it's because of all the attention he gets that you wish were yours."

"Oh, dear," Madame Balise said.

Randolphe grinned, the way a dog does when it is going to bite. He said, "You must admit that he does do a great deal to call attention to himself."

"So you think," Clarisse said coolly, "that what happened this morning is just his way of getting attention?"

"Well, it's working isn't it?" Randolphe looked around the table for agreement.

"You think everyone's suffering is just a ploy to get attention, Randolphe, and I suspect that that is your own truth that you impose on others. You resent our affection for him, don't you?" Clarisse was interrogating Randolphe now, and we could all sense his demise. I only hoped that once she'd accomplished it, she wouldn't, as usual, throw herself into his arms again.

"Well," he answered, "I think much of the time that it is human nature to try to get as much attention as possible, and these dramatic and exotic behaviors of his have kept him quite coddled and pampered."

"Quite cynical," I remarked.

"It's the truth," he responded.

"All cynics believe they are telling the truth. It relieves them from the responsibility and discipline necessary for hope and goodwill."

"Tell me, Randolphe," Clarisse finished, "why is it that with you the truth is always so dark and anything positive has some malevolent hidden purpose?"

"Because that's the way the world works, my dear. Because it's the truth."

Clarisse stood and pronounced, "That is your world and your heart."

"Tell Suzanne to bring more bread, dear," Monsieur Balise said to his wife.

Randolphe stood as well and, leaving the room, said, "That's right. It's all me. I am the devil and you are a saint, you whose hand gets caught in another man's pants."

"Wonderful green beans," I said. "I'm so glad the season has begun."

We all heard the front door squeal open and bang shut. Suzanne stood in the doorway with a tray of tarts that looked mangled.

As I was going home that evening, I felt an agitation in my flesh, a restlessness so severe that I could not imagine sleeping. But I wanted nothing more than sleep. Oscar fussed about taking my hat and bringing me the paper, which I let fall to the floor. Bending over, I put my head into my hands. Oscar asked if I was ill and I said, "I'm just a little dizzy, Oscar. I think I'll go out for a brandy." And so, five minutes after I had come home, I left again.

On the streets the gaslights were lit and there was a sheen on the stones from a fine mist, causing a man to sweat though it was still cool in the evening. Insects rattled, horse hooves clattered on the streets, dogs barked. I walked with my eyes closed, counting how many steps I could take without benefit of sight before a dizzying fear made me open them. I told God that I was putting my faith in him, that I would walk blind, surrendering to his protection. Ten steps–then eleven, and up to fifteen, before I gasped and stumbled to a tree for support. My forehead on the bark, I wept so that a baggy man asked if I was all right before asking for a few centimes.

I walked directly to a nearby café, where I ordered absinthe. It had been many years since my last indulgence, one that was regarded with pure disdain by most of my colleagues. They could explicitly explain its chemical components and the toxic effects of each one. I wanted the drowsiness anise provided and to be stupefied by angelica. I could not stop thinking of the Indian's death as a horrible sin that I and Madou had somehow committed. I poured the liquor through the sugar on the slotted spoon and watched it turn milky in the water. Still staring at it, I asked the waiter for a pen and paper. I wrote a note to Moulon, asking him to meet me at the Balise apartment the next morning to consult with me regarding what seemed to be an epileptic seizure. I gave the waiter the note and three sous to have it delivered to Charcot's house, for it was Tuesday evening.

Two prostitutes came in and seated themselves near me, nodding in camaraderie as they ordered the same poison. I drank my concoction, wincing at the metallic taste. In a few moments, I was at their table, explaining to them why I was seriously considering transferring my medical skills from the bedside to the laboratory. They listened well, before the three of us succumbed to a comfortable stupor, and I left as they ordered another drink for themselves.

I walked home with a sadness for the world, a deep regret and shame for the human condition and its delusions. "The answer is not cynicism," I told Randolphe, who appeared congenially enough in my imagination. "That is the coward's way, the spiteful child's way. The child who cannot love wants others not to love and so paints the world as dark and mean. I do not want that. I want to be a man, Randolphe, a man who tries even though he has failed time and again."

I saw a woman fondling a man, her hand in his breeches, on a bench in the Square Cambronne. I saw a cat crouched beneath a horseless cab. A female dwarf with a beautiful face asked what time it was. A gas lamp shattered and sprayed stars into the sky. I saw a large praying mantis's exoskeleton, headless, standing above the trees. I told myself that it was the new tower and laughed at the effects of the drug I had ingested, though I did not believe that I had had enough to stimulate my imagination that much. I still had my reason, and I was grateful and proud. But my doctor's voice told me to expect strange dreams, and I had one.

I was lying on the floor in the dining room of the Balise family apartment. Madou was holding my hand. I wanted to kiss her. She seemed exotic, though I was aroused only in an aesthetic way, full of affection. She offered me her breasts, which were exquisitely round and full, milk dribbling from her nipples. She placed one in my mouth and I drank, thinking that the milk was sweet, with no bitterness. As she held my head, with my mouth suckling her breast, she used her other hand to fondle the erect penis of the Indian, who was standing beside us. So intense was the pleasure that the whole building we were in started turning and then rose, dislodging itself from the earth and ascending into the clouds. Then I was alone in the cloud; the house fell back to the earth. I was amazed that the cloud was solid enough to carry me, and I was dizzy and lay down to keep from falling off. The cloud moved far above the buildings, trees, parks of Paris, over farmlands, vineyards, and then to the shore. It was night, and when I looked behind me, I could see dawn coming. I felt very happy and free. There was nothing beneath me but water. Then I was over land again. As the cloud floated close to a big river and hovered over a settlement of tents, I wanted to drop down, but I was still too high up. One of the people in the settlement below, a woman, looked up at me and laughed and waved. It was my mother. She was pleading with me to come down, to help her. But the cloud rose up again and went back the way it had come.

Over the ocean it was completely dark. I couldn't distinguish the water from the sky. There were no stars. I sobbed as the cloud passed over towns and farmland. I wanted to be with my mother. I could see the Place de la Concorde beneath me like a huge spider. Then the cloud descended and I was in my own bed, dizzy.

I awoke, pulled the chamber pot out from under the bed, and vomited.

It was an hour or so before dawn, and I knew I could not sleep again. I wrote the dream down, thinking that it might be of interest to one of Charcot's students, who was interested in the images of dreams and their neurological implications. The obvious effect of the dream was to disturb me. And I also felt an almost euphoric sensual longing. Then I muttered a prayer, kneeling at the window. I said, "Dear God, please let him be all right."

At nine in the morning I arrived at the Balise apartment, and a few minutes later Dr. Moulon arrived. Madame was quite upset because Suzanne had left, quit her service without insisting on the pay owed her–"packed her bags and left just like that, in the midst of our crisis."

Clarisse was taking up the breakfast dishes.

Monsieur Balise mumbled to me, "Bank business hasn't stopped, you know, . . ." as he put on his hat in the hallway.

Cecile and Madou were with the Indian, whose position had not changed. Moulon lifted Choice's eyelids, felt his neck for a pulse. He then asked the ladies to leave, and we proceeded to examine his entire body for rashes and discoloration.

"We should have his urine examined," he suggested.

"There is none to examine as far as I know, or very little, absorbed by the bedding."

Moulon left Choice's shirt and trousers unbuttoned and covered the man again. "He is perspiring," he said.

I responded, "Which is more reason for him to be hydrated regularly."

"There's no fever, no swelling," he said, feeling around the man's neck. "What about injuries to the head? The man could be unconscious because of the fall, the initial swoon having been a minor matter."

We examined his head for lumps and bruises, combing through the dark thick hair, which had been oiled by one of the sisters.

"I can't detect anything there," Moulon said.

We stood, Moulon sighing.

"I think he's done for," Moulon said.

"From what?" I asked.

"Don't be angry with me, my friend. I didn't push the man down the stairs. Who knows what head injuries he's sustained. We have no idea of his medical history, and you say he was sick as a child. He could have had some fever that damaged his heart. There's no diagnosis we can make until the autopsy."

"A grim thought," I said.

He put his hand on my shoulder.

"You haven't come around Charcot's lately," he said. "Goutier was there with his cello looking for you."

"I've been very occupied."

He nodded and said, "Apparently not at Hôtel-Dieu. No one's seen you there."

"I've been there," I said. "I've been in and out rather briefly. My private patients have been demanding."

"Well, I hear it that the famous writer won't have you cross his threshold, that you tried to treat him with your violin." Moulon laughed and went to the door.

I looked down at Choice and said, "There is no privacy in this city. I can just imagine what's been said about me."

"You're not all that important, Philippe," Moulon said. "Most of the talk has been about the exposition and the upcoming elections and Laborde's damned paper."

He opened the door and Madou immediately appeared in the doorway.

"What do you think?" she asked Moulon.

I spoke up quickly, "His lips are parched, Madou."

"All right," she said, "but what is your opinion, Dr. Moulon?"

I glared at him with such force I thought I might burn through his skull. Madou saw my expression and said, "Never mind. I understand. Philippe, don't insult me. I despise being protected by people who assume I am as weak as they."

"Well, Philippe," Moulon said, "I think she has dealt you quite a blow."

Madou came to the bedside and stroked Choice's face. She took the glass of water and sipped from it. Bending over the sleeping man, she touched his lips with hers and gently pushed water from her mouth into his. Two little streams came down the sides of his mouth. Madou straightened and said, "Leave me alone with him."

Moulon was gone from the room.

18

L'humeur sombre de la famille coulait le long de courants divers . . .

THE SOMBER MOOD of the household flowed along various currents, including Monsieur Balise's fear of the cost of a funeral for a stranger and his wife's concern with fetching a priest.

In the parlor, Clarisse was crocheting, her disdain for Randolphe strongly present as he paced in front of her. He was trying to interest her in a conversation about his latest plans to make his mark upon the world. He was going to write a series of articles for the newspapers on the whole matter of the Indian, in an anthropological tone. Clarisse ignored him and told her father that she would pay for the funeral herself.

"The man isn't even a Christian. What hypocrisy!" Randolphe said.

Clarisse, looking at her sewing, said quietly, "Randolphe, I think you should leave. There is enough to deal with here without your anger as another burden."

"I have to get back to the bank," Monsieur Balise said. "I hope this business is over soon, or . . ."

Randolphe put his face very close to Clarisse's. I stepped forward, ready to throw him out the window if even his spittle touched her.

"Go to hell," he hissed. Clarisse continued crocheting, her neck turning scarlet.

Randolphe left, passing Madou as she came in. She was putting a little green hat on; she had dressed up in some old finery, a green tea dress and delicate leather shoes. She was pulling on a pair of lace gloves.

"I am going out," she said. "Philippe, will you stay with him?"

I agreed to do so.

In the late afternoon, Moulon came by again with Dr. Laborde. Soon after they entered, there was a tremendous banging in the stairwell. Someone shouted, "Open the door," and when I did, I looked down at Randolphe, who was standing in front of a huge coffin, almost as wide as the stairs. On the other end was the apartment building's errand boy, looking very lanky.

"Where is Clarisse?" Randolphe asked.

"She is with the Indian," I answered. "Are you going to bring that thing up, just the two of you?"

"We're managing," he said, adding, "though it's mahogany inlaid with gold and marble and damned heavy." He said to the boy, "Come on then." Struggling, Randolphe had his back to us and the boy groaned as he pushed; the two managed to push the monstrous casket up a few steps.

"I have to put it down," the boy yelled, his voice cracking.

"Dear God," Moulon said, starting down the steps.

"You must lift it up," Randolphe said. "I can't hold it on my own."

The boy yelled, "I can't!" dropped his end, and fled, just ahead of the coffin as it slid down like a sled. Randolphe stumbled, just managing to let go of the gold handle at his end and fall to a sitting position.

"Do you know how much it cost me?" he called out.

Laborde muttered to me, "He must have stolen that thing from King Louis' tomb."

"Damned generous of you," Moulon said to Randolphe. "The four of us can get it up the stairs."

Laborde held up his hands, his bag hanging from one of them. "Not me. My back is weak."

"Let's carry the far end," I said to Moulon.

The coffin bumped loudly against the stairwell. I took the opportunity to say quietly to Moulon that I saw no reason for him to have bothered to bring Laborde, who had a tendency to diagnose everything according to his obsession with addictive poisons. "And he's brought his surgical tools. Whatever was he thinking of doing?"

Moulon only said, "He is interested in the case."

Someone from another apartment stood at the bottom of the stairwell and said, "What the hell is going on?"

Groaning, we made it to the middle of the stairs and stopped.

"Is someone already in here?" Moulon asked.

When we got the coffin into the hall, Madame Balise stood beside it, working her rosary fiercely.

"Oh, Randolphe, you are a saint," she said. "If only that poor man could see what a beautiful thing you have done for him."

"Where shall we put it?" Randolphe asked, standing straight with his hands on his hips.

"I think next to his bed," Moulon suggested.

We lifted the casket again, I feeling a growing sickness of the spirit. I thought of what Madou would see when she came into the room. "He cannot die," I muttered.

Clarisse backed away when we came through the door, putting the coffin through sideways.

"What is this?" she asked.

Randolphe spoke roughly: "You with your great intellect must surely know what it is, my dear."

"He is still alive," she said, backing up to stand in front of the window.

"I looked all afternoon for the best one I could find. The poor man deserves at least that after what he has been through in this household."

Clarisse left the room and Randolphe followed.

Laborde said, "Has anyone used the cups on him?"

"Whatever for?" I asked. "There's nothing wrong with his lungs, if you'd like to take a listen."

Laborde stated, "But you are doing nothing at all!"

"How can you have a cure without a diagnosis?" I said.

"You must do something," Laborde insisted.

"Why? Why must we?" My voice was loud.

"One must make some effort, man," Laborde continued.

Then Madou was in the doorway. "What is this?" she said calmly. "Is he dead?"

"No," I said.

"Then what is this hideous coffin doing here?" she asked. "It looks like a concubine's."

"Randolphe bought it," I explained.

Madou burst out laughing and then covered her mouth.

"I have something to tell him," Madou said. "Will you let me in?"

The three of us had been huddled near his head, since now the coffin took up a large portion of the floor on that side of the bed. We all moved around it to the foot of the bed, Moulon sitting on the coffin.

Touching the Indian's cheek with her lace-gloved fingers, Madou bent over and said into his ear, "You are going home."

Immediately, Choice's eyes moved under the lids. Madou straightened up and pulled at her gloves. Laying them carefully on the table beside the bed, she turned to Choice and smiled.

"Mr. Cody will send you home," she said. "It is all arranged."

As I was leaving, I passed on the stairway a man clearly of Choice's race, an indigenous fellow, taller than Choice, who said as he passed me, "I've come to see Black Elk," in English and then in French.

I said, "You must mean Choice. He is there. He is just up there."

"Thank you," the man replied.

19

Le cercueil a plu l'indian énormement.

THE INDIAN was greatly impressed with the coffin, stating that it was far better than what he'd probably end up in in America. In a long note I received a few days later from Madou, she explained the state of affairs in the Balise household: Randolphe was insisting that Choice's illness was a fraud, an act put on to get attention and to get what he wanted. He ridiculed the entire family for their complicity and set about, with the help of Monsieur Balise, to sell the casket for more than he had paid for it, which cheered him up considerably. In the last paragraph of the note she said, "Dear Tic-Toc, I deeply regret attacking you. You have been my dearest friend and I am ashamed of myself. Please come with us to the Exposition before Choice leaves for America. We are planning to go this coming Tuesday evening."

The Universal Exposition was, of course, all anyone spoke of. The huge area along the Champ de Mars, extending to both banks of the Seine, was transformed, along with the neighboring cafés, into a city within the city. The newspapers were full of celebratory pride. They included a few desultory lines about the contributions of other countries, including a brief description of Buffalo Bill's Wild West Show. My patient the Old Soldier praised the fountain of lights and the villages of exotic societies, evidence of France's success as colonizer. Competing bands played in cafés. I wanted no part of it. These displays that fed the masses, increasing their hedonism, irritated me. As a physician at the Hôtel-Dieu, I saw an increase in alcohol poisoning, gout, stomach ailments, and lacerations owing to accidents and fights. Crowds of people mingled and got into mischief, indulging a variety of appetites. Spectacle and intoxication crooked their fingers in the evening, when the heat abated. One man whom I treated had his nose broken outside the Retrospective Exhibition of French Arts because he had said out loud that the American artist John Sargent was more talented than our Millet.

I would have let this popular madness pass me by but for Madou's invitation. She met me at the door of her apartment, once again in the simplest attire and no jewelry. I told her that she looked like a nun on holiday. She replied, "I am paring down to the least possible affectations, Tic-Toc. If I am going to join Choice in the wilderness with his people, I have to give up the frills of my society, which is a great relief to me."

"So you are going with him?"

She looked around and came close to me in the little hallway. "Yes, I am saving my money, even asking for charity from my students to collect enough money to follow him. Would you buy a painting from me?"

"Madou, I was going to ask you to do my portrait. Will you? I'll pay for that."

"Yes! What a grand idea! You don't mind if I'm brutal with you?"

"I expect it. You must promise to reveal my true essence in whatever hideous way is honest."

"Oh, how grand! It will be my last portrait on this side of the ocean."

"And Choice is going right away?"

"Yes. Mr. Cody wanted him to join the show again. He even had a dinner for him, and everyone gave him three cheers. Of course the Indians wanted him to join the show. But Choice said something I will tell you, Philippe, but you must not ridicule it. Please do not mention it to Moulon and that group. I know how they would mock us."

I raised my hand as though to swear secrecy and she continued, saying, "He said that his soul had traveled back to his people and he saw his mother. He saw her face and how she needed him to come home."

She gauged my response and then continued. "He said that when he was lying so still, his soul traveled on a cloud over the ocean and–"

I stopped her. "I don't want to hear, Madou. Please. It's better if you don't tell me." I felt something pinch the inside of my skull. "It disturbs me somehow. It's all . . . it isn't rational, you see . . . I . . ."

"Mr. Cody bought him a ticket home; he's a very kind man," Madou said. "I'm going to follow soon." She whispered this last statement, and I asked her if her parents knew her plans and she shook her head.

"I've had an interview at the Pasteur Institute," I told her.

"I'm glad for you, Philippe. It seems that we are finding our way, freeing ourselves." She embraced me, and we held each other for a moment. "You will miss Paris," I said.

We were silent for a moment, and then she said, "Come have coffee at the table. There's pudding tonight; the new girl made it."

The table was unusually calm. The new woman, large and silent, brought in perfectly baked crème brûlée, the glazed crust on top a delicate ice on a creamy pool.

Clarisse, Madame Balise, and Choice were listening to Monsieur Balise talk about the suicide of the assistant manager of the Comptoir d'Escompte, owing to the falling prices of copper, which ruined his bank and him. Monsieur Balise said, "He and others are ruined not so much by the vicissitudes of the economy as by too much desire to appear rich before one is rich. The lure to appear rich causes people to go bankrupt, buying on credit, giving profit to others for showy trinkets. I tell you, the only true power is to have money, not to appear to have it. That's what the bourgeoisie don't understand, and they let their ignorance be exploited. They parade their false wealth while the truly wealthy hold the power. If they only had any sense . . ." He chomped down on a spoonful of pudding, having, like me, saved a piece of sugary crust for the last bite.

I agreed wholeheartedly with his philosophy.

Madou said, "I am more interested in a personal kind of power, which sustains one more securely than finances."

"And what gives that power?" Clarisse asked her sister.

Madou said, "It is the ability to be alone, to be alone and strong. In that case one is never with someone else out of desperation."

"Oh, that sounds bleak," Clarisse said. Madou shrugged.

Monsieur Balise, bored by the path his daughters wanted to take in the conversation, said to me, "And what, as a man of science, do you believe gives one power?"

"Well," I said, spooning up whatever I could of the streaks of pudding remaining in the cup, "I believe it is to see what is rather than what one hopes or fears is." I refrained from pontificating on the noble efforts of Thucydides as compared with the passionate blindness of so many of our philosophers. "Power for the man of science rests in being willing and able to observe clearly, to devise a theory from the facts and not try to make facts fit a theory."

Choice laughed and pronounced a phrase I heard him utter often: "Hech too allo." Madou had told me it meant, in effect, "It is so indeed."

Madou stood up and said, "Come on. I want to go before it's completely dark."

When we were in the hall, Clarisse interrupted us to say that she was going to come along. "The four of us again!" she announced.

Choice was behind her, dressed in his best Italian suit and top hat, laughing at himself. Two braids again lay on either side of his chest. Before going into the parlor, Madame Balise breathlessly warned us about pickpockets, hypnotists, and cheap goods. I peeked in to say good evening to Monsieur Balise before we left. The entire parlor was covered in Madou's paintings; they were on the mantelpiece, on the floor, leaning against the furniture. There were at least four large portraits of Choice's face in a variety of colors. Monsieur Balise was deeply involved with his pipe and didn't see me. While he was tapping it against the fireplace, it broke in two. I quickly retreated before he could see me and heard him mutter, "By Jesus."

The four of us left gaily, Clarisse chatting about how Randolphe had sent her a note that day saying that he was ready to forgive her for making him a cuckold and that he would even consider marriage. "I am trying with all my might to stay strong. I am well aware that I am far more content when I have loosened his hold on me. But I am still in need of constant distraction so I do not find myself on his doorstep begging."

"I had no idea the man even had a doorstep," I muttered. "It's as though he pops up from the ground like Beelzebub."

Madou said to me, "Clarisse has even gone with Cecile to one of her doggie meetings."

Choice was quiet, a gentle smile on his face, and he teased Madou and made affectionate gestures, such as pressing his nose against her hair and whispering to her. They tended to walk ahead together, looking as French as the other lovers, lost in each other's fragrance and voice.

Clarisse suggested that we stop for a refreshment in the Café du Tambourin before getting a cab to the Champ de Mars.

The place was crowded and smoky, a collage of black hats and feminine frills, waiters' aprons and tinkling cups and glasses. We sat at a table with a mirror along the wall above it. We had to speak loudly to hear each other. When the waiter came, Clarisse said, "I'll have an absinthe."

"Oh, no, Clarisse," Madou said, her nose wrinkled. "That is such nasty stuff. Tastes like copper and puts one in such a stupor."

"That's what I want," Clarisse said.

Madou ordered a sherry and Choice asked for coffee. I said, "I'll have cognac."

We drank in silence, comfortable enough with each other to look around at the others in the café and give our opinions of them.

"Oh, there is that horrid poet. He is quite the addict," Madou said. "Oh, Clarisse, I can smell that awful stuff. How do you abide it?"

"I mix a lot of sugar with it. I like it," her sister replied.

Madou then turned to me and said, "So, Tic-Toc, what do you think of my paintings?"

Choice stretched, an amused smile on his lips.

I stared at her, trying to make her question disappear. The café had suddenly gone quiet, it seemed. Clarisse, Choice, and Madou looked at me, waiting. Then Madou reached out her hand.

"It's all right, Philippe, just tell me. Do you think they are really that bad? Worthless?"

"Who am I to say anything about art?" I could not look into her eyes.

"How terrible do you think they are, Philippe? Very bad?" She was clearly fighting against anger, with a still, small smile curling her lips up slightly against their will.

Clarisse said, "Oh, Madou, don't torment him."

"Why didn't you tell me before? Why didn't you just tell me, instead of pretending all these months?"

"I was not pretending anything," I protested.

"Oh, please!" Madou banged the table with her hand.

"You didn't ask me," I tried to explain.

"That's shit!" she said loudly, and the couple at the next table looked at us. "Shit! You should have said something right away, you and your shit about seeing things as they are. I suppose that doesn't include telling people what you see, telling your supposedly close friends. Oh, you are so closed. I cannot stand it!"

She stood up. Choice pulled her back down. She sank against him, glaring at me. I almost expected her to put her thumb in her mouth. I had seen children whom I had given medicine give me the same look from their fathers' arms. Clarisse laughed.

"They are a process in themselves," Madou explained.

"When I paint them I'm engaged in a kind of ritual. I can't explain it. It's quite enough. That's a difficult thing for anyone to understand. There's so much wanting to be noticed in this society."

When the waiter came around again, Clarisse ordered another absinthe.

"You'll make yourself sick, Clarisse," I said.

"No, I won't. I just want to make an evening of it! We're going to the grand exposition!"

Madou and Choice wanted nothing more, and the waiter began to leave, but I called out, and when he turned I said, "I'll have an absinthe, too, this time."

Madou said, "Don't abuse yourself on my account."

Choice cleared his throat but didn't speak. The absinthes arrived, and Clarisse and I looked at each other like two contestants in some sporting match. We drained our glasses. I finished first and ordered another. After finishing that one, I stood up, my head swirling as I adjusted to a new perspective.

"Let's go!" I said.

"This is not like you, Philippe," Madou said.

"Well, you're going off to the Wild West, you who cannot walk a mountain path without whining like a child, and are going to join the Indian tribes and skin bison when there are no more bison, and Clarisse has finally rid herself of the Prince of Darkness, and Choice, my best assistant ever, is abandoning me. This seems like the occasion to deviate from normalcy. In fact, at this moment, I find normalcy infuriating, as though it might choke me."

Clarisse looked up lazily and laughed.

"Yes," she said. "to hell with normalcy! We will all die of it!"

Madou said, "Listen, I don't mind about your honest opinions. Just don't patronize me by hiding them, all right? Never again."

"Never!" I said, saluting her.

The world outside was yellow to me, and I began to speak in my head as two characters. One was the Dr. Normand who carried his bag and the other was the Dr. Normand who carried his violin. The first man noted that the effects of the absinthe included a distortion of the retina's intake of image and color. The second man told him to stop being a bore.

20

En nous approchant de l'exposition, nous fûmes submergés par un fleuve humain.

As WE APPROACHED the gates of the exposition, we became a current in a river of humans. Music from different cultures and bands came and went as we passed. Faces looked into other faces for a mirror of their own moods: merry, awed, serious, weary, drunk, disappointed. All classes and ages talked, pointed, laughed, fought: children cried for more, older children sulked, vendors yawned. Entertainers from Java, Indochina, Algiers, and other exotic colonies walked briskly by; parcels were dropped and retrieved; and a man yelled that he'd been robbed as people strolled past him.

"We should all go to Mr. Cody's show," Madou said. "We could surely get in for free."

Choice shook his head.

"I think he's had enough of that sort of thing," I said to Madou.

"An old dream," he said.

We stopped and tried to find an activity that the four of

us could agree on. People jostled us. There were clouds of various colors in the sky. A man dressed as "Lady Liberty" was standing just inside the gates yelling about France's injustices in Indochina. People were throwing balled-up newspaper pages at him. Madou refused to see the exhibition of paintings.

"I am not up to hearing Dr. Normand's opinions on art tonight," she said.

The discussion became frustrating to me, and so I walked off, leading our little group to the Historical Exposition of the Revolution. In a hall with a stage, our exiled emperor was presented in heroic fanfare by means of vignettes wheeled before us. The pomp and exaggeration made me laugh, which caused several strangers to shush me. One vignette displayed a group of Prussian soldiers pulling a woman by the arm as a stuffed dog in a perpetual snarl threatened to bite one soldier's leg. When the stuffed dog fell over, Choice and I burst into laughter at the same time; one man in the front row stood up and turned toward us, yelling, "See here–show some respect!" We were quiet, but I could see Choice pinching his nose hard to keep from laughing, and then I had to bend over. Little sighs escaped as we continually failed to stop ourselves from a new fit of laughter, until Clarisse hit me in the arm and said, "Let's get out of here." When we got outside, Choice and I fell against each other, moisture squeezed out of our eyes as we laughed loudly.

"It isn't that funny," Madou said. At least she was smiling. Clarisse was dismally agitated and said, "I want to go home." This changed Choice's mood, and he patted Clarisse on the back. He led her over to a bench where the two sat.

Somehow it had become dark, and Madou said, "Let's go see the fountain. Come on, Clarisse. We must see the fountain."

A large crowd stood around the spectacle of lights near the great tower. It absorbed me. I was enchanted. There were hundreds of illuminated jets of water. The colors changed from orange to red, green to blue, all melting into one another. These streams of water and light and color filled the air. I could not look away. I was certain at that moment that God was light. I felt giddy, elated. Madou clutched my arm and said, "Oh, Tic-Toc, I have never seen anything so beautiful." And I looked for Choice, because I suddenly had a pride in my culture, in the wonders, both potential and realized, of technological genius and artistic ideals. I wanted to tell Choice that God could manifest in human endeavor, especially in work that honored light. The Dr. Normand holding the medical bag was about to tell me that I was delusional, and I wanted Choice's assistance. He was looking up at the tower, studying it.

Clarisse moved away, and Choice followed her. Then Madou and I, silently awed by the lights we could still see reflected in the faces of the people we passed, kept up with our companions.

The long Esplanade des Invalides was a row of displays of the places that France had conquered. Cochin, Tonkin, Annam, Senegal, Algeria–all the exotic cultures now proudly under France's flag in the process of being transformed into museum displays. Men beside little chariots that they pulled people around in called out, "Ride in ginrickshaw?" We passed by clusters of bamboo cottages. Choice stopped to watch a troop of Javanese girls dance. They were aliens, people of another planet entirely, fantastic in their helmet-shaped headdresses, heavy arm bracelets, and exquisitely embroidered garments, which wrapped around them from their armpits to their ankles. Their bare arms and shoulders moved like liquid when they danced. And the dance was subtle, coy, and peaceful. They pulled a sash from one shoulder to another, making cries like kittens while their sisters played instruments made of reeds. A small drum kept a steady, hypnotic beat, as one man played music on something that looked like a crude Irish harp. Something made the beautiful droning noise of musical glasses.

The richness of the world overwhelmed me. Choice took me by the elbow and led me to where Clarisse was leaning against a tree. She looked at me, and I felt as though she were down in a pit, though we were standing together on level ground.

I heard Madou's voice behind me say, "What's wrong with her?"

Clarisse sobbed and said one word: "Randolphe."

"Is he here? Has he done something to her?" Madou said.

Clarisse shook her head, and Madou in disgust said,

"Oh, for God's sake, Clarisse. Look at all there is to see here. Randolphe is an addiction for you. There is no other sense to it." She walked a few feet away, and Clarisse looked at me and said, "I'm sorry. I want to go home."

I felt like a boy who was about to be forced to leave the carnival, which he would never see again. I refused to be Clarisse's doctor. The thought of her pulling me back into my adult persona as a doctor made me angry. I wanted to slap her. "I want to see the technological exhibits," I said.

Choice carefully pulled Clarisse from the tree and walked her along the path. I ran to Madou and grabbed her hand. "Come on," I said, and ran with her. I didn't care if we lost Choice and Clarisse. But Madou protested, laughing, "Wait for them, Philippe."

I asked people along the way to tell me where the great globe was. We passed the caves of troglodytes, wigwams, the Hindu palace. "I want to go there," Madou said.

I pulled her along. "No. Come on. I'm not leaving without seeing the globe."

In one of the science and technology pavilions, we found it: the large, three-story-high replica of the terrestrial globe. Many people, all silently walking up and down a spiral gallery, studied the slowly turning representation of the planet on which they lived. One could walk beneath and all around it, until standing above the North Pole.

"Look, Madou," I said. "There are the pathways of ocean vessels, and look, even all the railroad tracks all over the world. Magnificent!"

Several people had stopped in the middle, one man saying to his wife, "I had no idea there was so much water."

"Yes," Madou said to me. "Philippe, there is so little land. Look how vast the oceans are. Is this accurate?"

I nodded, but had to admit that the proportions were shocking.

She pointed with her finger, making a line in the air that went from France to America. "At least it isn't the other ocean," she said. "This one is rather small in comparison."

Choice was merrily showing Clarisse the path of his travels. By her own gesture, I could tell that she was indicating to him the place of Christ's crucifixion.

"Very far," Clarisse said, and Choice stared at the place as it turned slowly away from him.

Clarisse moved away from him, too, back down the ramp toward Madou, and said to her, "My heart is pounding. I think I'm sick, Madou. I am so afraid."

"We'll leave soon, Clarisse. Won't we Philippe?"

I ignored them both and walked beside Choice. We stood together. Here was the world, and here were he and I before it. I put my arm around his shoulder. He spread his hand out in front of him, wriggling his fingers to indicate all the different colored dots that were all over the globe. It was decorated with hundreds of them.

"Holy places," he guessed.

I shrugged. It seemed unlikely that this was the case, since there were so many dots. I stopped a man who was alone and had an educated deportment, and I said, "Excuse me, sir. Do you know what those dots indicate?"

As it turns out he was an Englishman, but he understood me and answered in both languages, "Those mark the world's mineral deposits." He looked at both of us and rubbed his fingers together. "Great wealth." He lifted his watch out of his vest and pointed to the solid gold back of it and repeated, "Great wealth. Great potential!" Grinning, he made the motions of digging.

I found the information interesting. Choice leaned far over, waiting for the globe to turn to his homeland. His hand was poised over the land of his birth, where there were many colored dots.

When he stood up, I saw intense horror on his face. And because I had just been looking at the little colored dots, when I looked at his face, it was covered with them. His mouth trembled, blue, green, red, yellow dots on his skin.

I thought, "Dear God, he's going to have another spell. He's going to die."

Slowly, his head hanging down in thought, Choice walked down the ramp and outside. His deportment had completely changed. He pushed through people, staring ahead, shaking his head a little as though to tell someone, "No."

As we gathered outside, Choice kept walking. We left the park and walked past the cafés. Choice was ahead of us. Clarisse suddenly stopped, looking into a café window, and said, "Dear God, it's Randolphe!" She burrowed into a crowd of people and entered the café. Madou called out Choice's name as we followed her sister. The inside of the café was a smoky mass of noise and faces. A band completely composed of women was playing in that café. They were dressed like gypsies. The leader played the violin and wore a white dress decorated with gold braids. A thick braid of her own black hair beat against her back as she played her violin. The other girls in the band wore short, dark blue dresses and red jackets. They played a Strauss waltz as the voices in the café laughed, yelled, called out for Tokay or cognac. Madou grabbed Clarisse by the sleeve and pulled her out. I stayed behind, loving the music, the boldness and exotic costumes of the women playing it. I clapped vigorously when they were done; a strange woman embraced me and kissed me on the cheek. Then Madou pulled me from behind by the waist of my pants.

"I thought I saw him," Clarisse repeated to me when I was outside. Her whole body shivered as though she had been plunged into ice water.

The boulevard shimmered with gaslight and music and café life. Madou's voice was in my ear, saying, "We'd better go. Clarisse has completely come apart. Where's Choice?"

Choice was ahead of us. He had stopped to wait but now resumed his walk at a distance. The gas lamps radiated a rainbow of colors. Beneath them I could see tulips that seemed to pop open as I passed.

"I am in love, Madou," I said. But she didn't hear me. Choice was walking backward now, waving at us. Then he started clowning, running backward in a winding pattern. Three men passed us, and one handed me a glass of champagne. I drank it and threw the glass over my shoulder.

Clarisse clutched my arm tightly. "Everything is so strange," she said.

"Yes, and it's fantastic," I said, wanting to shake her off, but I had a feeling that if I did, if I were cruel to her, I would lose my intoxication and have to crawl home through shadows. Resentful of her imposition on my gaiety, I let her burrow into my side.

"This place is exquisite, Madou," I said. "I don't think you can leave it."

"It is an exquisite monster," she said, "an arrogant, exquisite monster poised to eat up the world."

"But look at this, Madou. Look at this right here–not generals and businessmen–the music and art and lights, the effort to be as alive as possible."

"You mean the effort to be as intoxicated as possible," she said, squinting to still see Choice. "There's a large difference."

Choice was continuing to clown, stepping in and out of the gas lamp, still running backward as he got farther and farther away.

And then he was gone.

"Take care of Clarisse," Madou said. "I'm going after him."

"You can't wander around the city alone at night," I called after her.

She called out, "Isn't it exquisite?"

And then I was alone with Clarisse, and suddenly there were no cafés, just the river, empty and liquid beside us. I imagined the letters from Clarisse's lover, Madou's paintings, my medical instruments, banknotes, corpses of tribal peoples–all carried away by the river.

"I'm sorry, Philippe, to be such a bother," Clarisse said.

"It's all right," I said, though my euphoria had completely evaporated.

21

Cette nuit toutes sortes d'images défilaient dans ma tête, pendant que j'essayai de dormir.

THAT NIGHT a variety of images played behind my eyelids as I tried to sleep. I saw colored lights, colored dots, gypsy women, tulips; I felt that my bed was rotating like that accursed globe. Unable to sleep, I looked out my window, where I could see faint reflections of the exposition lights and the steel shadow of the tower. I sat in a chair by my bed and rubbed my face.

I became alert when I heard voices in the other room, whispering voices. I stood and listened, my heart racing. There was soft laughter, a woman's laughter. I imagined that Oscar was kissing the neck of his laundress in my parlor. I put on my robe and opened the door. The room was dark, a little light coming from the street lamps below.

There, sitting in my reading chair, was Choice; Madou sat at the table, her gloved hands in her lap. They both looked at me and smiled.

"Did we wake you?" Choice asked, in perfect French.

"No," I said. "No . . . I was awake."

Madou said, "Come and sit with us." She got up to give me her seat, and she sat on Choice's lap.

I obeyed and then said from my seat, "What are you doing here?"

I looked over at the pile of bedding in the hallway. As far as I could tell, Oscar was there, undisturbed, or he was gone and had left his bedding in disarray.

"I wanted to talk with a colleague," Choice said, with a somewhat teasing tone. I felt I needed to be on guard.

"Where have the two of you been?" I asked.

"Oh, we've been to church," Madou said. We could not fully see each other's faces in the dark.

Choice said, again in perfect French, "We were in the big church. I wanted to go there, to think there, to understand whatever spirit empowers this machine that churns out white men and sends them all over the globe like a female frog producing egg froth."

This was an unpleasant image. I wanted to see the face of this man who sounded like a Frenchman and had the shape of Choice.

"Give me some light," I said, reaching for a stub of candle lying on the table. I lit it and dripped wax on the saucer, then affixed the candle to it. I saw Choice's hawk nose and dark eyes as I pressed the hair back from my forehead.

Choice nodded and then leaned forward, shifting Madou, who was resembling a sleepy rag doll. He said, "I have a question for you."

I shrugged. "Go ahead. I'm aware that this is a dream. Ask what you like."

He asked, "What god do you believe in?"

I sputtered, "What a question! Well, I believe in a god. God. I suppose . . . Well, I'm not a religious man."

He said, "Listen. I'll tell you what I've figured out. Now I know why the Spirit of Everything had me stay here so long, until I thought I was going to die here. I figured out that this spirit keeps sending messengers, and people keep not hearing what they're saying. Magical beings have been sent to tell the truth, but then people start yelling and waving their hands around, explaining what the messenger said and fighting about it, calling other messengers with the exact same message demons and enemies. It could be funny if it didn't cause so much suffering."

Madou yawned and made a nest of him, curling against his chest. He held her firmly and said, "When I go back, I'm going to join every church there is. I'm going to participate in all the rituals there are, because it all comes down to the same thing. The only difference is whether or not one listens to the message."

I wanted to go back to bed. Madou looked so peaceful there in his arms.

"It's late," I said. "I'm tired. I don't want to have this dream anymore."

"People pray to God, constantly talking. Talk, talk, talk–but they don't listen to God."

"We'll sleep here. I don't want to move," Madou muttered.

Choice put up one hand and bowed his head in a parody of a magician about to reveal a vision.

"I see Napoléons, thousands of Napoléons, like ants, with books and money and machines in their hands." He sighed and added, "Whew! Look at me! Now I'm a chatterbox just like a white man! It's a good thing I'm leaving!"

Madou was asleep. He held her, sinking back into the chair. He put his face into her hair.

Madou looked so real. I reached out and touched her cheek. It was warm; I combed my fingers through her hair.

"Am I dreaming?" I asked him. "If I'm not, I can sleep out here. The two of you will fit better in there in my bedroom."

And he answered, "We don't need your bed. We're not real. You're dreaming."

I laughed and looked at him, wanting confirmation that he was not joking. He raised his eyebrows and laughed silently, jiggling Madou a little.

"But I wanted to tell you before I leave that in my community you would have a place of honor as a wink-tay. I wanted you to know that." He closed his eyes and sighed.

"Wink-tay," I repeated. "Well, thank you."

I stood up and went back to bed, feeling nauseated.

In the morning, both Oscar and I were very grumpy. I asked him if he had let two people into the apartment the night before.

He said, "I wasn't here, to be quite honest. Did you forget to lock the door?"

"I don't know," I said.

I forced the candle stub off the saucer and rolled it on

the table and then asked, "Do you believe in God and Jesus and all that?"

He answered, "I don't see why I shouldn't. It's wiser to believe and be wrong than not to believe and be wrong."

"Very reasonable of you," I said, still rolling the candle stub around. "You're a veritable Pascal."

I finished my coffee, dressed, and left the apartment, taking my violin with me.

22

Je n'ai jamais repris d'absinthe.

I NEVER DRANK absinthe again. In the days following, I imagined Madou preparing herself with trunks and bags to follow her man across the ocean to the American wilderness. In only a few weeks I left my position at Hôtel-Dieu and was hired on at the Pasteur Institute. I continued to drop in to see the Old Soldier and the Widow. To Oscar's delight, I moved into a larger flat, near the Place de la Bastille, away from any view of the giant dead tree. The flat had a kitchen, and so I hired a cook. Oscar detested her, called her an insult to French cuisine, and left me. I saw him waiting tables at a café near our old flat. We spoke like old friends.

In November I was happily surrounded by beakers and burners and dry ice and cages of mice. I thought of Cecile whenever I passed the cages of dogs down the hallway from my laboratory, which even I could not abide seeing, smelling, or hearing. In fact, I made the mistake of turning my head enough to see a little beagle standing up, wagging its tail, and looking at me from its cage. Once our eyes met, there was no hope for discipline. It was not a rational act, but I hid him under my coat and took him home. I would have rescued them all and wondered if I had become a misanthrope and given all my affections to what are incorrectly called the "lesser" animals.

Choice once told Madou that a man must prove he is not a coward before he has the right to ask a woman to be his wife and have his children. I fear that under such a rule, 90 percent of the marriages in Europe would be annulled. I thought of him often, sometimes as he was, and sometimes as the colorful faces of all Madou's portraits. She had never painted my face, of course.

I dreamed of him quite often, once with a blue man unfurling inside him and occupying his skin. I daydreamed about Madou riding a horse, shooting guns standing up on the horse's back. I could not stand the idea of dining at the Balise household without Madou at the table.

But then I received a note from Clarisse that shocked me. Madou was not riding on the back of a horse across the prairie. She was in Salpêtrière, across the river just a few minutes away from my new apartment.

When I went to see her there, I asked her first what they had subjected her to, for I was more strident than ever in my assertion that the more "science" that was applied to the human spirit, the more harm was done. It was my increasing conviction that the scientist must be a servant who diligently uncovers the chemistry of suffering and humbly admits when the suffering has nothing to do with chemistry. It seemed to me, as I walked through those doors after years of avoiding the place, that Salpêtrière was a monument to human fear–the fear of the doctors and the patients. In that place, controlling one's emotions became an absurd increase in suffering.

Madou was calmer than I in explaining the methods that had been employed to shock her from her "madness." Hydrotherapy had been used, as well as hypnotism, which only made her laugh.

"Madou," I said, holding her precious face in my hands. "You simply must convince them that you are not ill. And the best way to do that is to praise them for their reason and confess that all they have done has been successful. Sometimes one must lie in order to be free, one must weigh honesty against freedom."

"They are considering removal of my ovaries," she said.

She was standing, leaning against the wall and staring at me. "I want to get out of here, Tic-Toc. It's not a good place. I don't see very many people, but I can hear women calling out. It's bad for the nerves."

"I will talk to Charcot. He is not a brute. He will set all this straight. Perhaps you can go to America, Madou. I'll . . . I'll even go with you myself."

"It's all right, Philippe. You don't understand." She sighed and told me: "That last night that we were all together at the Exposition I caught up with him and followed him all the way to the Île de la Cité. He went into Notre Dame. We stayed there for hours; the swallows that are caught inside flew back and forth, and he told me that this was a holy place. He said that there should be a globe that marked all the holy places."

Tears came into Madou's eyes as she said, "He told me that one day the dead tree would bloom, but it would take a long, long time. You know, I'll admit that I wondered for a moment if he were not mentally deranged after all, but I loved the strength of his arms, the firmness of his voice, all used so lovingly with me.

"But even so, I had the oddest knowledge that I wasn't going to be his wife, that he didn't want me to go with him. It was sad, but also a great relief, because I knew how strongly he loved me. And I knew, as you did, that I could not skin a bison, whether they exist or not.

"When I took him to the train station, I told him I would follow soon. He didn't say anything, but he held me for a long time. He held me very still for a long time on the platform. Oddly, Philippe, when the train left the station, I felt free of something. I don't know what.

"Father and mother were so cautious, so afraid when they greeted me at home. They were afraid I was going to fall apart like Clarisse. But I was calm, pensive. I went into Choice's room to paint. After a few days, Philippe, I . . . well, I saw Choice. I saw him. He came to me. He made love to me. And so it has been, except for when I've been in here. He comes to me and we are together. I can't say it any other way."

"Madou, are you saying that you have dreams of him?" I asked.

She smiled wearily and said, "If that's how you must have it, Philippe: I have dreams."

I squeezed her shoulders, lifting her so that her face was in front of mine. I hissed at her, "Do you want to get out of here, Madou? Do you? You cannot tell people that you have sex with a man who is thousands of miles distant!"

"Oh, but women do it all the time," she hissed back.

I let her go. "You don't understand . . . ," I began.

"I do understand," she answered. "Believe me. I've learned to slant the truth. I told my parents, you see. I told them, when they asked, why I was so happy."

"Why on earth did you tell them? Your father is a banker and your mother goes to church every day!"

"Because I love them. Because I want the people I love to know who I am!"

I was exasperated. I told her my true thoughts.

"Perhaps you are insane, Madou," I said.

She said, "Perhaps I am. And perhaps you are, too, for conversing with two apparitions in your apartment about God and Napoléon."

My body went hot, in an electric way. Madou laughed.

"The new girl–you've seen her, Tic-Toc: she is huge, as large as a carnival strongman–she held me while father fetched a cab and enlisted a policeman to escort me here. And here I am."

"Who is sane, after all," I muttered. "And we always thought that Clarisse . . ."

"Oh, no, Clarisse is quite sane! She and Randolphe are married!"

When she saw my shock, she laughed and nodded. "Yes," she said. "Mother was delighted. And there is already a child on the way."

"And Cecile?"

"Oh, she is devoted to dogs still, and I suspect her of lesbianism. She goes to the Café du Rat Mort at night."

"I have thought of her often," I said. "She would approve of me now, I think, since I have rescued one of the dogs from the institute. I named him Sadi, after the president–hid him in my coat."

There was an uncomfortable silence as we both realized, without having to say so, the irony of my having freed the dog while Madou was imprisoned here and I had made it clear that I should not help to free her.

"I cannot fit under your coat, I'm afraid," she said kindly.

Nether of us spoke for a moment, until I took her hand and said, "Come on, Madou."

She said, "Philippe, you could lose your position. I understand, really."

I pulled her to the door. "Come, Madou."

The troglodyte who was sitting at a desk in the hall was talking to a doctor, a man I didn't know. Someone was banging hard against a door near them and they were ignoring it.

Madou's hand felt boneless and cold in mine. The doctor saw us walking down the hall and said hello. That was all. Then he continued the conversation with the other man and the banging on the door went on.

And that was the extent of the challenge, though I understood that when Madou was found to be missing, I would be implicated.

"Perhaps we should leave town for a while," I said when we were on the street, blinking against the sunlight. The boulevard seemed so intensely normal, so safely occupied with its trivial business played out in huge dimensions.

"Philippe, you have done something very courageous," Madou said to me. "Choice would say that you have earned the right to marry."

I laughed and said, "Yes. You saw what a fierce fight they put up."

Madou and I went together that day to Chermoutier, to the little inn owned by the German and his wife. In Reims I bought clothing and toiletries for both of us. I showered her with luxuries. In Chermoutier, I told the German couple that we were married. Madou and I stayed through dinner and lay together for the whole night in the room that Choice and I had occupied. We held each other fully clothed.

"I don't want to betray him," Madou said to me.

"I understand," I responded. And then I asked, "What does 'wink-tay' mean?"

We could not see each other's face in the dark, but I could feel her pull away and put her back against my chest. She pulled my arm over her waist and put my palm against her lips.

"It means 'wants to be like a woman.' "

I took my arm away and lay on my back. In a few

minutes I went out onto the roof of the shed and sat until dawn. For some reason, the sun coming up made me laugh.

I had to leave that morning and suggested that Madou stay there for a while. When I returned to Paris, I wrote a number of notes. I made up a series of stories explaining her absence from Salpêtrière. I even went to the Balise household and consoled her parents, who showed remarkably little concern for Madou. They were more stimulated by the impending birth of Clarisse and Randolphe's child than by anything to do with Madou. I did not see any of her paintings, and I politely declined an invitation to dinner, though I could smell the chicken roasting in wine. I felt that I had nothing to say to them any longer, that I was not the person they thought I was. In fact, I was never that person, and I was weary to death of all pretense.

When I came across Madou in Paris many months later, she was riding her bike and dressed like a Hindu. She had a red dot on her forehead and was wrapped in a green cloth that draped over her head. She wore leggings of the same material and Roman sandals. She told me she had met a teacher, a man from a Hindu land, and she lived in a house with him and others learning his mystical truths near the Luxembourg Gardens. I didn't ask about Choice. I felt that she had gone mad in a quiet way that was beyond my reach.

The next year, Buffalo Bill's Wild West Show came

again to Paris. It was there for several days, and I went every night, alone. I studied each one of the Indians' faces, but Choice was not there. I saw Rosa Bonheur packing up her paints and easel one evening, and before I could ask her if she had seen Madou, she asked me if I knew if Madeleine Balise had gone to America.

"No," I said. "She is still in Paris."

"I haven't seen her in a very long time," she said.

"Her paintings are quite remarkable," I told the woman, whose romantic portraits of the showmen seemed insultingly empty of passion. "Mademoiselle Balise's portraits are works of genius," I said.

"Perhaps," she responded kindly. "But she is unschooled."

The Balise family disappeared from my life for many years. I went to their apartment once and found them gone. A frayed woman sweeping the steps told me that they had moved back to the eighteenth arrondissement, where a larger apartment was more affordable. I stayed on at the Pasteur Institute and often worked in the evenings, sleeping on the couch in my office. I heard news from time to time from Moulon, who had married a wealthy daughter of a marquis. He had become one of those doctors of the demimonde who charge high fees to attend to the courtesans of the nobility. He stopped by the institute to chat with me about our mutual acquaintances. He told me about a woman who had been one of

Tourette's patients and had tried to assassinate him, claiming that he had taken control of her mind through hypnosis. Tourette himself was in the dismally obvious advanced stages of syphilis, and his friends were conspiring to get him into an asylum. Moulon came to see me one evening to tell me about the matter and then mentioned that he had seen Madou at her sister's funeral.

"Funeral!" I felt that someone had pushed me in the chest.

"The middle sister," Moulon said. "The married one. Very tragic. You know the Baron de Mackau horror."

"She was in the fire?" I asked.

"Yes. She and her husband. He survived."

The whole world knew of the fire. A tent had been set up to display a new entertainment, a fantastic technology called a kinematograph. There had been notices all over town promising a spectacle of moving images, including a Wild West display of cowboys and Indians. I remembered thinking then that Choice and his people were finally caught in a technological amusement, just like those ragged, lost people of the French colonies at the Exposition.

Hundreds of people crowded into a tent set up by the Baron de Mackau. The machine caught fire. More than two hundred people burned to death, mostly women, including the Duchesse d'Alençon, the sister of the empress of Austria. The British papers made quite a storm over the eyewitness reports that the men of Paris ran out, leaving the women in their billowing fashions to burn.

The Baron de Mackau, who organized the bazaar, was sentenced to a year in jail. I wanted to find Randolphe and kill him.

"How did Madou look?" I asked.

"She was very sad, of course. But she was gentle with her mother."

"How did she look?"

"What do you mean?"

"I mean was she dressed as a Hindu?"

Moulon thought and answered, "I'm not sure what a Hindu dresses like, but she seemed quite normal to me, but unmarried still, and wearing a black dress like her mother and sister. I still find her quite attractive, you know, though she has reduced her fashion to its simplest form, almost like a nun. Still, there is something exotic about Madou that piques one's curiosity. But I doubt she will ever marry. She is a spinster now, after all."

"Yes, she is, I suppose." I wondered if Madou considered herself a spinster or a holy woman who had sex with a phantom, and then I asked, "Was the sister's husband there?"

"Oh, yes, making quite a show of his grief and clutching his children, more like a child himself than a father. And her father is quite feeble. I detected a serious heart condition. Madou held him firmly and sweetly. She seemed to be a sturdy comfort to her family. Her sister's children strained to be with her."

I shook my head; I could not bear the images of Clarisse's hair in flames, her skin broiling. It was horrible.

Moulon put his hand on my arm and said, "I'm sorry. I thought you might have already been told. I talked to Madou. I asked her how she could abide her sister's husband, with all the rumors about him and the other men running out. And do you know what she said, Philippe? She said, 'The poor miserable man. He has always been miserable.' She told me that it isn't the abused who are as much victims as the abusers, who are unable to contain the volume of their misery, and they keep adding to the misery with the shame of their actions. Can you imagine? She is far too easy on the man. I wanted to beat him to death right there myself."

We both sat in silence until I said, "Yes, that is just the kind of thing Madou is capable of saying."

"She is such a child," he said.

"But it is true," I told him. "I would not want to be Randolphe. Would you? I would rather have been Clarisse with some strength added. In fact, I'd most like to be Madou."

"You would like to be a woman?" Moulon asked.

I looked long into his eyes, large brown eyes, and said, "Yes. I would like to be a woman."

He smiled, then laughed, then punched me in the arm and stood up.

"I think you ought to marry her," he announced, magnanimous in giving up his own infatuation.

"Yes." I said. "Yes. I think you're right. Yes, I think Madou and I could protect each other's serenity, and that is, after all, what two people who love each other should do."

Moulon had lost interest and politely left. The day's edition of *Le Figaro* that he had carried in with him was on my desk.

The Americans were poised to invade the Spanish island of Cuba in their hemisphere. France had intentions of making a great naval base at Bizerte. War between Germany and England seemed highly probable because of German breaches of international law in central Africa.

When Madou and I were married, I bought a globe for our parlor. I now scour books about all the cultures of the world, searching for mention of sacred temples, sites where miracles have occurred. In fact, I consider my own place of work as one of them, for it is the place responsible for a miraculous reduction in the suffering of this world caused by diseases of the tissue. Diseases of the spirit I must leave to others. I have put a pin on the place where Jesus died. Slowly I am covering the globe with little pins to mark the cities and geological formations where one might feel some healing of the spirit–most of them places that I will never see but that I must know are there and unmolested. And I am happy to think that there are many I will never know of and that no book or museum or anthropologist or speculator will ever study, like that spot on the lake where Madou watched as I and the Indian swam together naked.

One night I dreamed that the steel tower on the Champ de Mars bloomed, blue flowers unfolding on it. Everyone stopped to look at it, suspending for a moment a cruel comment, unclenching fists, thousands of people putting down some item they had meant to buy but suddenly realized they didn't need. When I awoke I felt very old; I felt that if I died, I would not mind. And if I lived for a long time, I would not mind that either.

AUTHOR'S NOTE

In 1887 Buffalo Bill's Wild West Show went to Europe to perform for Queen Victoria's great Golden Jubilee: the celebration of her fiftieth year as Queen of England and its growing empire. On board the ship that sailed from New York harbor was a young Lakota man whose name was listed as "Choice" and who was later to be known as the great medicine man of the Lakota people, Black Elk. This young man was one of hundreds of Native Americans hired by William Cody to provide the "extras" for his Wild West show.

When the ship left England to sail back to America, Black Elk and another Lakota man were mistakenly left behind in Sheffield. Desperate to get home, Black Elk signed up with Mexican Joe, who had his own, cheap version of Cody's spectacle and who was touring Europe. In his famous talks with John G. Neihardt many years later, the old healer Black Elk briefly mentioned his homesickness in Europe, where he eventually, in 1889, took refuge in Paris with a woman friend and her family. In that same year, Paris's Exposition Universelle put on an extraordinary celebration of the white man's power in industry and colonization, symbolized by the building of the Eiffel Tower. A year later, in 1890, the Lakota people were attacked by the United States military at Wounded Knee, South Dakota. They surrendered and were massacred. The Buffalo Bill show continued to tour in the United States and Paris, where the public was enchanted with cowboys and Indians and had no news of the massacre at Wounded Knee. Black Elk has since become a respected archetype of the Lakota peoples and of the enduring wisdom of shamanic warriors.